MURDER IN at DIGO SPRINGS

NANCY TREU KLOTZ

★ SterlingHouse Publisher, Inc.   Pittsburgh, PA

MURDER IN at INDIGO SPRINGS

ISBN-10: 1-56315-415-3
ISBN-13: 978-1-56-315415-7
Trade Paperback
© Copyright 2008 Nancy Treu Klotz
All Rights Reserved
Library of Congress #2008924346

Requests for information should be addressed to:
SterlingHouse Publisher, Inc.
7436 Washington Avenue
Pittsburgh, PA 15218
info@sterlinghousepublisher.com
www.sterlinghousepublisher.com

Broadmoor Books
is an imprint of SterlingHouse Publisher, Inc.

SterlingHouse Publisher, Inc. is a company
of the Cyntomedia Corporation

Cover Design: Brandon M. Bittner
Interior Design: Kathleen M. Gall

Printed in U.S.A.

DEDICATION

Everyone regardless of race, creed or color
needs to implicate themselves in the work for justice,
it's policies and practices,
to see that it is resolved fairly at all times.

To my friend, Ruth

Nancy Irene Klotz

CHAPTER 1

Without warning, a crackling sound interrupted the morning stillness on the pine needle path Jim Benet traveled. Jim's sudden action of looking back caused his horse to rear. Retaining his seat he rode forward a few feet and looked all around at the changing trees and red berry bushes. The sound puzzled him. He looked down and to his amazement found two sets of horseshoe tracks.

"They don't look new, boy, maybe a few days old. Somebody must have been here earlier. There are only a few dried tracks and no footprints. Not too much to go on. Whoever came couldn't see Sam's house from here. Maybe this may have been somebody's meeting place. Sure is curious, though."

When he decided to resume his travel to Sam's house, two squirrels jumped in front of him. Jim felt a sigh of relief, thinking the sound may have come from them.

Jim could see Sam's small wooden house in the distance through the pines. He sat taller in the saddle, easing the stress he felt in his back and muscular frame. He shrugged his broad shoulders and thought about seeing the men he needed to help him in his cause.

What was it going to be like this time? Would another argument develop when someone expressed an opinion not in agreement with the rest of the group? Who would draw his gun?

He had had a premonition for some time that the outcome of this session would turn into an argument again. Frankly, he thought *it scares the living hell out of me. The last time I could have been killed had the words run amok and the trigger pulled.*

He recalled the discussion with Frank, Sam, Tom, James and Judah about obtaining the railroad for the community. They had conversed for over two hours, and while talking, Sam held up his whiskey bottle and attempted to make his point.

"I don't think this community is ready. We gotta build up our good points first and make sure the people understand." Then he swallowed his homemade firewater. "Tell the council...."

"Wait, Sam," said Jim. "We can think of all the reasons good and bad as to why the community isn't ready. If we wait any longer, we'll never get the railroad."

James stood up, wobbled a bit, and said, "What do you mean, never?" He pointed at Jim with his bottle. "Sam's right. What do you know? You came here from another country."

"Yes," said Jim confidently, making a fist with his right hand to make a point. "I came from Scotland, and as long as I am here, I will help where I can, and in this railroad business, we have to make a decision."

"No, we don't," said James, with his body and legs weaving trying to find his balance and drawing his gun at the same time he clung to the bottle. He pointed the small pistol at Jim.

Jim's body stiffened. "Wait, James. I don't carry a weapon, remember?" The men arose as quickly as they could except Sam, who had trouble standing.

"No harm meant, James. Why, there's noth'n to it," said Judah.

"Now, let bygones be bygones, ol friend," Sam muttered still trying to stand.

"Now, look, James," said Tom. "We don't want you to be sorry for anything. And you're right. We better wait for a suitable time to come. Jim meant no harm. You know he didn't."

James stared at Jim, who was still visibly nervous.

"Now, James," said Frank slowly, reaching down to James' gun hand. "We can settle this peaceably. Let's meet another time when we're all settled down and have had time to think about this railroad business."

James smirked, putting the firearm back in his pocket. "I don't like the word, *never*. 'Till another time, Jim," he said falling back in his chair.

Jim thought seriously about what the statement could mean, including his own behavior, and tried to remain calm in the face of adversity. He felt gratified that the men had spoken up. He remembered shaking on the inside and hoping and praying that his last breath would not come at any second. What happened? What caused this sudden change in everyone, or was it a change? Maybe now Sam, James, Judah, Tom and Frank wanted to make this meeting up to him in a friendlier manner. *Well, we'll see*, Jim thought.

Before riding forward to Sam's, he promised himself that he would try again with everything in his power to ensure the community's future and make certain it could not be destroyed by those who were uninformed and misguided in their thinking. Jim reasoned aloud, "I know I can convince people their community has a future and would be able to advance; however, this area will have a future only if certain people can let go of the past." If only, he repeated to himself as he quietly meditated for a moment and rode closer and closer to Sam's porch.

He caught a glimpse of Frank Fuller's horse tied to the post and puzzled to see that neither Tom Turner, Sam's inseparable cousin, nor his two closest accomplices, James King and Judah Arnold, had yet arrived. Jim wondered what caused their delay. What was keeping them?

Jim edged cautiously down the path, getting nearer to Sam's house, watching for anything to happen or someone to appear. He saw nothing and no one. The door was open.

The aroma of food that drifted from inside the house into the morning air made Jim aware of his hunger. He rubbed his stomach and became distracted by the scent. With his salivary glands warming up, he hoped the meal would be served before the meeting. Then any serious discussion regarding the railroad would not be interrupted.

Sam appeared in the doorway, smoothing his unkempt jacket and pants. He smiled. His eyes glowed around his dark beard with speckles of white; it seemed thicker than usual. His shoulders stooped slightly as he leaned over to grab Jim's hand with his only arm. He did not seem tense as he sometimes did to Jim, and his smile broadened as Jim sauntered toward him. Jim thought he smelled alcohol on his breath as Sam spoke to him in a friendly tone.

"Come on in; you're late. All the hot food's gettin cold. Frank's in the other room. Lottie got the food ready before she went to tend the store. By the way, how are you?"

"Good. I've been wondering how you've been feeling. Have you…?"

"Jim," said Frank, rushing into the parlor. "I'm glad to see you. How's Lauren?"

To Jim, Frank appeared healthy. His rugged complexion from hours in the sun and his big calloused hand which grasped Jim's hand tightly, gave the impression that Frank was clean cut. Jim noted the gray in the temples. As usual, Frank carried his favorite pipe in his pocket, ready to grasp it at any minute with his only arm.

"She's feeling better, thanks. You and Betty owe us a visit," replied Jim.

"We'll come as soon as we can. There's a lot of work on the farm, and I'm sure you heard some of my help left, so I'm short-handed. No one wants to work anymore, so I pitch in. You know, since my accident. I'm still trying to get used to one good arm," said Frank, as he rubbed his empty coat sleeve.

"You never do," said Sam, who waved for them to sit at the table.

"Oh, the table is only set for three," said Jim quietly. No one replied as to the whereabouts of the other invited guests.

While the men sat down, Jim kept going over the proposals for the railroad in his mind and how the men would interpret them for the community. He realized he should have sensed their hostility the last time the group met. Jim felt deep within that they were not going to change their minds or make concessions for the town.

"Jim, what are you thinking about so seriously?" asked Frank.

"Oh, just listening. Pass me that stew," said Jim. "I'm hungry."

Jim did not really listen to what was said till after the meal. He always knew he was a third party when Frank and Sam were together. Each man had lost part of his left arm. Sam's was amputated during the battle at the Rapidan-Rappehannak line at Richmond, while Frank lost his below the elbow in a hunting accident on his farm. Back at school in his native Scotland, Jim met his friends from America, Frank and Sam. He knew they were close, since they had grown up together in Indigo Springs.

"Jim, what have you been doing with yourself? Rumor tells me you studied the law very hard," said Sam, talking with a mouthful of food.

"You're right, I did study very hard. It paid off in many ways," said Jim.

"What do you mean?" said Sam, devouring a big piece of meat.

Before Jim could answer, Frank said, "Why, he means just that. When you get an education, it pays in many ways. Right, Jim?"

"Sure," said Jim, who was concentrating on other thoughts. He recalled both men helped him get to America and soon after to Abbeville, South Carolina where they gave him letters of introduction. For this, he was grateful but still concerned as to how he fit into their friendship. What would happen to this friendship of many years? Would it remain strong, or would they lose respect for each other? Jim understood his kinship to them. He felt a part of the lives of Frank and Sam, but he could tell from the time he met them that they were akin to each other, committed and compatible. He decided to find out just where their thinking lay and take one more chance.

Jim believed that both men's experience of losing an arm brought them closer in thought and deed than they had ever been before. Sam rarely removed his coat when people were present because some women would utter sounds of dismay and whisper to their partners. This intimidated Sam. Jim remembered being told that Sam had just come home from the war and stood in what was left of the doorway of his mother's house looking for his wife, Lottie. He removed his coat and did not see his mother's old slave, Jessie, standing behind the broken staircase.

"Massa Turner," Jessie said in astonishment. "You look like you was in a terrible way. Why, you ain't got your other arm!"

"Where's Lottie? I want to see her? Where is she? Answer me."

"Now I's free. I don't have to fetch her no more, and besides I's too old and my back hurts me. Miz Lottie's in the back field." Jessie pointed in the direction.

"Well, I'm younger, but my arm is hurt'in me. Get her or I'll see that you don't leave here," Sam bellowed. "That's how I lost my arm, and if I have to loose the other one defending my house and honor, I'll do it!"

Jessie could see his left arm was no more than a short stub. "I'll get her," she replied as she watched her former master with downcast eyes and knew the look in Massa Turner's eyes spelled hate. She eagerly ran to get Lottie.

The loss was an adjustment for both men, especially for Sam who was subject to moodiness and irritability. Jim thought that Frank seemed to take it in his stride after a while and pacified himself by smoking his pipe and concentrating on his farm.

"All right. No more small talk. Let me lighten this meeting with a bit of good news, since you almost asked anyway. Don't you want to hear it?" said Jim, waiting for a reaction to his statement and studying both mens' expressions.

There was silence and a look of despair, as though they did not like being interrupted.

"First, I am announcing that yours truly passed the bar. I just opened my office in town and thought you both might want to come and see it. Lauren did a fine job in decorating it. I'm really excited about practicing law." Jim waited.

"Well, I thought I'd get some sort of reaction. You know I've persisted. Been studying for a long time. It paid off! I can assure you, I am elated!"

After a moment, Frank said, "Congratulations!! You took me by surprise. I thought this would happen next year. You've accomplished your goal! I knew you would since the day of our first meeting. You're that kind of person."

Sam smiled and looked pleased. "This is truly a great occasion," he announced and got up to reach in the cupboard for a full bottle of whiskey.

"Wait, Sam," said Jim. "I only want…."

"Sure," said Sam. "Just a toast. Take the top off."

"But there's more," said Jim as he pulled the cork for Sam but didn't take a drink himself. "I wanted to tell you that as an attorney now, I am serious about helping this area continue to grow, and definitely one way would be through the use of a railroad, the issue we discussed before. It would bring growth to the community, manufacturing, and better education…."

"Jim, hold it right there," said Frank. "Sam and I have been discussing this since our last meeting, and we agree you're going too fast with your plans." Frank shook the tobacco from his pipe. "We don't believe this community is out of a bad situation yet. You know how the war has affected all of us. In fact, devastated us. Jim, you saw this when you arrived in Cokesbury in

1868. You saw our burned homes, the children and women sick and depressed, the horrible feeling of defeat all around us, and most of all, the sadness of our loved ones gone forever. Everything was taken from us. The corrupt legislature seemed to forget us many times. It will take a lot of money to get this railroad. Money this community and its citizens don't have."

"Frank, I am convinced times are getting better," said Jim, jumping to his feet. "It's 1877! Sam, you and Lottie agree your store's beginning to thrive, the community's come together and people are mingling with each other and communicating. They are looking to better times. The sick look of war and disease is fading. There's hope now! It's our future, our community's future. Governor Hampton, the man we hoped for, is now in Columbia. He's a forward looking man for South Carolina. He has our interests at heart, and I know for a fact that the railroad is a part of his campaign strategy in the days to come." Jim paused. He walked over to Sam and looked him straight in the eye. "Think of what we can do if we get the railroad!"

Frank shook his head. For a moment no one spoke.

"Well," said Sam as he took a big swallow of the golden liquid. "Hold it right there." He held up his arm. "I've been working on this railroad business for a long time, and I am convinced we're ready for a railroad, but only when the community is ready, and it's not ready yet. Our future changed drastically before 1865, but the federal troops have not completely gone yet. Our profits are eroded. Now, the only thing we can do is play a good game of politics with the town council; that's all. Then we'll get our wish."

"Look," said Jim, sitting down. "Both of you know your families have established a good community here. It's solid!

We've also a few prosperous farms again. That's a plus. Now, we've got some in the community that are still struggling, and the railroad can change that for the poorer farmers like the Franklins and their helpers, the Davids, the O'Neils and Bob Nickels, if he ever gets back."

"Wait a minute," said Sam. "We're not getting the railroad for just the farmers. We need it for everyone. It's going to take us places and open up the South again."

"That's the idea!" said Jim. "That's the idea."

"But, Jim, you've got to think of the fact that the farmers who live in Indigo Springs are tight-fisted, especially folks like Drusilla," said Sam. "You can't even talk to her. She won't give a penny, and the Davids who work for her and her brother, George, haven't a dime either. We've got too many people like that, and I'm going to drink to my statement. Here's to you."

He held up the bottle and took two swallows.

Frank's chair was near the window, and he motioned to Sam. "It looks like Tom."

Jim's heart skipped a beat. He had hoped Tom and his friends would never show up.

"Oh, wait a minute; it's your helper. Looks like he wants to see you, Sam."

Inside Jim sighed relief and continued. "Well, Sam," he said as Sam slowly went out the door. "I'd like to help farmers like them any way I can, as in land disputes and similar cases, but in looking around the community, the townspeople have problems too, like money matters in families and pensions from the war. Then there's the poor who need advice and assistance, and the railroad could help."

Jim approached Frank. "By the way, Frank, since Sam is

outside, where are Tom and James?"

"Sam said earlier that they would be here."

"What about Judah?" asked Jim.

"I'm sure he'll be here too. He doesn't want to miss any excitement."

"As far as I'm concerned, the later the better."

"I am inclined to agree."

"Frank, is everything all right with Sam these days?" Jim glanced nervously at Sam. "He seems to be drinking again and a bit edgy about everything. What's gotten into him?"

"Oh, I think Sam's just too busy. You know, too many things to do," Frank said. "Confidentially, he and Tom bought a large piece of property in North Carolina."

"My goodness! You say a large piece of property. How big? Is he going to live there?" asked Jim.

"Don't know the size of the land," said Frank as he watched outside for Sam to come near the door. "He didn't really say. When you arrived this morning, that's when he started to tell me."

"That's interesting. His store business must be picking up. Takes money to buy land like that. Maybe he made a little extra on the side, gambling, although I do wonder what he is going to do with the land. Got any ideas?"

Sam entered the room. Frank did not reply.

"Well, men, have any decisions been made yet?" asked Sam.

"Not exactly," answered Jim. "Let me toss this next thought of mine out to you both. How about including the poorer farmers in the discussion about the railroad? Maybe some of those names mentioned before like the Franklins and the O'Neils of

Indigo Springs and others there would have something to say. Let's hear their opinions as well."

"What are you thinking?" said Sam as he took a few steps toward Jim and flung his liquor bottle back and forth. "They haven't got a notion of what to do! Take George, for instance. He worked for my parents once and caused more trouble than anyone. He always complained. There's not a lick of sense in his body, and besides, that sister of his, Drusilla, runs his life. The whole community knows they are misers."

"Now," said Frank calmly, "let's give that idea some thought. It might have some merit politically. After all, they deserve a chance to say something, just like my help."

"Then let's be at the town council meeting in about a month," said Jim. "Let's talk to several of the councilmen." He rose from his chair, ready to leave before the men changed their minds. "I am convinced it will do some good."

"I'm not sure I can make it," said Sam bluntly.

"There are problems for me too," said Frank, "but I'll be in town for a few days prior to the meeting, and I'll put in a good word to the councilmen I see about the railroad."

"I'm going to make it," said Jim, "and do everything in my power to move this proposal on the railroad right along. Sorry that neither of you can make it. Sam, thanks for the meal and hospitality. Tell Lottie how good it was, but I best be on my way."

Jim went to the door, and to his chagrin saw that the riders he dreaded meeting were coming steadily closer. "I see some friends of yours, Sam, riding this way."

The men looked up and saw Tom, James and Judah riding in. Sam headed for the door bottle in hand. Jim had already gone out.

"Well, Jim, we'll talk later," said Sam, shouting so Jim could hear.

"I'm tired of talking. I want some action," replied Jim. "You can't blame me for that."

Jim grabbed the reins of his horse. He got on the saddle and watched the riders come Closer, three abreast. Their grim expressions gave utterance to Jim's fears. He sensed they were coming for him. The premonition he had earlier came back. Who would draw his gun? Frank was still inside. Sam clutched his whiskey bottle and waved at them calling, "Hey, hey!"

"Well, sir, you're not leaving!" said James, quickly dismounting and looking directly at Jim. "I expected to find you here. I hope we're not too late to express our humble opinions and add to your great discussion of getting this railroad to our credit."

"I'm on my way. I have business at my office," announced Jim with determination.

"We heard you got a new place in town, all that poundin' and paintin'," said Tom. "I hear it's right nice."

"Yes, I like it. Come by and see me, Tom, so I can be of service to you on any legal problems you might have."

"Heck, I got no legal problems. Just a bad stomach and back. Hurts most of the time. Ol' Doc Waddle wants me to go to a doctor in Columbia."

"Tom, you should go," said Sam. "The pain you got seems to bother you—turns you cross."

"Now, we discussed that before, and I told you I'm not…" said Tom firmly.

"Hello, Tom," said Frank. "I can hear you complaining way in the house."

Jim turned his horse to ride off. He replied, "Anyway, gentlemen, I must be going. I do have an appointment at my office, and if I leave now, I'll just make it back in time."

"Wait," shouted James.

Jim's body cringed at the command from James. What could happen now? He turned slightly, his body inside shaking. What did he want?

"We want to discuss the railroad. I've got a good proposition that will make us rich. Don't you want to hear it?"

"Sorry, I must be on my way," said Jim. He spurred his horse and galloped off.

When Jim felt safe and far enough away from Sam's house, he looked back. He saw Frank galloping toward him. Frank soon caught up with Jim, who slowed down for his friend. They rode side by side for a few minutes until Frank broke the silence. "Don't give up on us, Jim. We need you because no one else has our community's future in mind like you do."

"Frank, I'm not riding off because I feel this is a hopeless situation, but it is useless to keep on trying to come to some agreement with Sam's continuous drinking and James' get-rich-quick schemes, and what I perceive to be a lack of interest in progress by the other party. Were you sent to try and convince me?"

"Yes, I volunteered. As you heard earlier, I agree with Sam and the others that in a year or two the community will be more open to new ideas again, and the railroad will be a part of our community then, but something more important has come to my attention. Since you are an attorney, I think you should know about it."

"Frank, you say in a year or two. Actually, what does that

mean? We are not the only town vying for the railroad. Green-wood is competing also. Where do you think the money will come from all of a sudden? Who or what will bring in the goods?"

Frank looked dejected but said, "Well, Jim, on the whole, the community does the best it can. Going faster for this or that reason doesn't make the answer right. We need more time."

"All right. Time is running out. It's over 10 years now. You mentioned something has come to your attention. What is it?"

"You know I am on good terms with my ex-slaves. Some stayed with me, and I help them whenever I can. But they've come to me this time with a perplexing problem and want an answer. They are like kin to me, and I said I would try and help them. Their faithfulness and hard work carried my family through the worst of times and enabled me to keep my farm when others lost theirs. Anyway, they said they want a rally for their politician who is coming into the Cokesbury station soon. A gathering like that could cause trouble. I suggested they hold the rally inside their church and not congregate at the station."

"Just what kind of trouble are you talking about, Frank?"

"Sam said they'd get riled up from all the ideas the politi-cian would put in their heads. Maybe start a riot. What's going to happen is that this politician would like to be close to them. They'd depend on him to get them land and special privileges. We do that for our kin, you know, relatives and friends. We'd do it for each other, wouldn't we, Jim? But this man may not end up the best influence. That's what bothers me."

"I'd say give him a chance," said Jim. "Hear what he says first, then take action. What ideas do you suppose this man has? Is he some political wonder? You know, President Hayes has just about moved out all the federal troops, so for him there may not be much protection."

"Long before the war he used to work for my mother. His name is Randolph Harris. He ran away and got into local politics on the coast after the war. From what I hear, he wants his followers to get stronger politically and get involved in demonstrating in groups," said Frank.

"That's admissible, isn't it? Certain needs in everyone's life have to be met, or there are problems," said Jim.

"But, Jim, you know what a close community we are, and it has taken this place and its people a long time to finally restore their homes and feel normal again in family life. I don't want to see any more suffering."

"I don't want to see people suffer, either," said Jim. "Remember, I came here from Scotland. We fought the English, and there was pain on all sides. I want to help. I'm an attorney. I can help. Send one of the men you've been talking with to me. I'll advise him on what to do for the rally. Everyone knows there's room to grow now. That's why I stayed, because when there is room to grow, there's expansion; then opportunity knows no boundaries. This community can do anything it wants, for its future is insured. Look, you and Sam have your reasons for needing me, whatever they are, and I have my reasons, too, for needing you and Sam, but not the rest of the men. With them nothing will come to fruition. They have more to gain by stirring up trouble. I don't want to be a part of it, and my advice as an attorney would be for you to do the same."

Frank rode for a few minutes in silence.

"Look," said Jim sympathetically. "I'm sorry we can't come to some comfortable level of thinking on these issues. In all ways, what you do for your help is commendable, but on second thought, you better tell Sheriff DuPre about this. In addition, we've been friends ever since school in Scotland. You and Sam told me about this place. Don't you want to see this community grow? Be more prosperous than it was? You and the citizens have that opportunity."

"Of course I do. What makes you think I don't? I am just against any more suffering. Because of the loss of my arm my opportunities are limited. My chance for advancement in life is continuing to farm my land. All I can do, is to make it productive. Without it I would be worth nothing, have nothing. Each man must work his land to the fullest, or he'll let others down."

"But we will be letting the others down if we stay a farming community," insisted Jim. "We need the railroad to bring in the goods and take them out. That's opportunity. If pain and suffering come with it, so be it; but I know that isn't true. All some of us want is progress."

"No, Jim, that's politics. There'll be plenty of that."

The men rode a short way, not saying another word. They stopped their horses again and faced each other.

"Jim, try to see this railroad business our way just for a little while longer."

"Let's try to work together at the town council," said Jim. "Please make every effort to be there. It will signify to the council a willingness to work together."

Frank could not look Jim straight in the eye. Instead he nodded his head once, and waved his hand and rode off in the direction of his farm. Jim bowed his head for a moment, and led his horse down the dense pine forest path to another road home. *Is it possible for Frank to change his mind? He treats his help with a child-like affection. Where will these problems end? In fact,* Jim pondered, *how will I even begin the argument for the railroad without their backing?* He wondered again if his premonition was true. *Wait and see,* he thought, *wait and see. Each day brings something different! Wait and see.*

For part of the way, Jim followed the path he had taken to Sam's house. He came to the same area he had crossed before and wondered if the squirrels would make noise again. Jim thought of the hoof prints he could not identify before and looked around the path for them. To his surprise he saw several new ones. Were these the riders that came to Sam's house? Jim got off his horse and studied the hoof marks. They were indented in the ground as though the riders and horses had waited awhile.

"Well," said Jim. "They missed a good meal. Yet I wonder what their motive really was in waiting and what were they waiting for?"

CHAPTER 2

The dreary October night cast darkness over the land. It stretched through the tall pines into the distance where no eye could see. No rain or wind or mist touched Indigo Springs this night. In the stillness, Jeff wondered if he would go crazy waiting for the strangers to arrive. He rubbed his hands. He thought this visit by strangers resting in his cabin was something he normally might not take on. The church folks begged his wife, so he had no choice.

He sat down close to the window in his rustic one-room cabin. He put his face to the glass and peered out. His wife, Mandy, dozed in a chair, and his son, Jasper, watched the Franklin property outside from the sand hill so there would be no disturbance. Jeff desperately wished for peace within himself. He clasped his hands together. *Oh, God, give me peace. Don't let anything upset Miz Drusilla and Massa George!*

He strained so he could see through the layers of darkness hanging over everything. After all, Jasper was out there, waiting for the men and looking over the sandbank. If only he could see through the darkness, he would know all was well. A good time to stay inside, he thought. The darkness could penetrate the noblest of men who ventured out this night, causing them to fear their own heartbeat. It could also bring relief to anyone who sought refuge in the dark evening hours, which the three strangers sought.

The blanket of dark clouds would be an appreciated cover for the small party of three black men on horseback. Jeff knew they would soon slip silently into his cabin at Simms Cross Roads. They anticipated waiting there most of the night, then riding to the train station. One of them, a politician, would speak at the planned rally in the Cokesbury station. Jeff wrung his hands. He stopped when he noticed Mandy watching him.

Suddenly he said, "What if da plans don't work? What if somethin' goes wrong? The men were sworn to secrecy, but da white folks might recognize the politician. Oh, God, what'll ah do then?"

Jeff sat down in a homemade chair and bent over cupping his chin in his hands. The chair wiggled as he sat complaining to himself about the expectant visitors he did not know. He remembered his father doing the same thing many years before when situations got too stressful. Jeff surmised that this habit was a sign of old age.

Mandy looked at him from the stove, shaking her head. "Yous makin' something more than it is. Best hush now."

She kept her sight on Jeff who was short and muscular, with slightly stooped shoulders, had smooth dark skin like his Indian mother. He had a strong willful mind, like his black father. Characteristic of his Indian mother, though, he had premonitions of coming danger. These forebodings made his stomach churn, especially at the thought of food. This feeling would not allow him to eat anything all day.

The forewarning bothered him. He wrinkled his brow and rubbed his head. The muscles and joints in his body ached more than ever, although his work day had not been unbearable. Jeff traveled to town with some crops and brought back the money, which as usual, he gave to Miz Drusilla.

His thoughts were interrupted as he looked up, wearier than before, and saw the incoming men. He arose as fast as he could and spoke softly to avoid being heard by the Franklins in the cabin over the sand bank.

"Come in quick. Rest yourselves by the fireplace."

Jeff regretted that some of his agility was gone as he watched the men sit down by the fire. Nevertheless, he was proud of being a hard worker and not missing a day of work. Every morning he promptly reported to his employer's cabin to start a fire and haul the water, the first chore of the day.

The biggest man present sighed "Ahhhhhhh" from the fatigue of his journey. He let his body sink into the floor as if it were soft mud. He smiled as he felt the welcome heat of the fire. The man stretched his long legs till the bones cracked. His large frame seemed to drink in the coziness of the flames. His body relaxed and he yawned. Jeff and Mandy stared, somewhat taken aback by their visitor.

With a broad smile, the heavier man said to Jeff, "Name's Randolf Harris. They's my helpers. What be the name of dis place?"

"Indigo Springs."

"Why sure! Dis be the place where they made the blue-blood dye. I 'member breakin' the vats for firewood after da war. Been awhile since I come back here," he said with a chuckle. "Miz Fuller used to make it, 'cause she had a friend in the low country showin' her how. She wanted special clothes for her son in school somewhere." He paused and hit his knee. "She shoo me off her land."

Attuned to his own words, Randolf did not seem to notice that his companions were asleep. He chuckled again. "Since ah' be such a big man, somebody traded me for hard work. Ah made mah own way and ah'm still doing it. Ahs seeking re-election again as a representative in the legislature." He looked at Jeff inquisitively, "What you do here?"

Mandy took the cue since her husband did not answer and brought some fried rabbit and biscuits with hot coffee. Of course, Jeff wished he could eat. His stomach made noises he hoped no one else could hear. *Ah's afraid of having Massa George find out ah used his house as a place of refuge*, he thought. *Ah knows some of my friends want somethin' better in life. Ah knows my family is satisfied. Ah's too old anyhow ta risk losing what ah got now. No way will ah take chances on bein' carried off in the night, never to see my family again.*

Jeff suspected that the politician would not be able to remain quiet, hushed like a bird in his nest at night. He was right. The other two men stretched out by the fireplace and dozed, seemingly comfortable on the floor. Time passed, and Jeff watched the big man having a difficult time getting himself situated. The politician wiggled to the left and to the right and twisted and turned. "Mah foot's asleep. Oh Lordy! What'll ah do?"

He moved closer to the warmth of the fire and yawned, stretching again and wiggling his body. Jeff was amused at the man's loud gestures and could see by the firelight that Randolf looked tired. He must have traveled a long and arduous journey.

Jeff moved his chair closer to the politician and spoke with a finger over his mouth.

"You gotta be quiet lest Miz Drusilla hear you. We'd be in trouble."

"What you owe those people?" asked Randolph pointing in the direction of the Franklin cabin. "You oughta get what's comin' to you. Me, ahs made my plans for all the people. We's gonna move on up. We's got to, and that's what's gonna be said at the rally."

"Hmmm, it's fine you and those willin' to face things that will happen, but no one here's got the fortune or the youth or the strength to keep goin'."

"What you suppose we's gonna face? Why, we's facin' opportunity," said Randolf. "It's beautiful! We're gonna do a political turn-around. Got to. There's folks out there with nothin'. We're gonna live classier. Ah figure we can work on the Constitution next makin' it better for everyone. It's the next big thing. Some folks call it bein' equaled."

"Mista Randolph, you can talk all you want, but ah's satisfied. The Franklins take good care o' us even in the bleak time, but it's getting' better, and they treat us better. They was never mean or beat us."

"We's gonna pool our resources. We's gonna buy da land and divide it amongst us. It's not a bad plan."

"Mista," said Jeff, exhausted. "Ah'm supposed to see that you're led to the safest place in the forest come dawn, so's you can cross the land to the railroad faster. That's all. If ah goes any farther, ah be in trouble."

"You makin' a mistake not thinkin' 'bout your tomorrow."

The door opened. Randolf and Jeff glanced up and saw Jasper come in. His eyes glistened in the fire light. Randolf saw he was a tall young man who appeared about 15 with the eager expression of youth on his face. His light creamy complexion and high cheek bones rounded out a handsome physique under an old faded blue jacket and black hat. His long legs, thin boned hands, and lean body indicated the youth could run fast.

Everyone stopped talking. They waited for Jasper to say something, but Jasper looked at his father first. Jeff nodded his head.

"I looked hard over the sand bank. I watched the Franklin cabin. Nobody stirred," said Jasper, looking at each man. He glanced at his father and said, "There was no noise. I took the horses way into the woods and tied them up. But don't you think we should be going? Right away! Right away!"

"Come here, young man," said Randolph, who put his arms around the boy and hugged him.

Jeff was touched by his son's enthusiasm. "Ah agreed to let him accompany your party to your meet'n place. Come here, Jasper, so's ah can tell you something." Jeff whispered, "You only go as far as the edge o' the woods. When the signal comes, ya come back. Ya hear me? Don't step out in the open."

"Yes suh."

Randolf ate the fried rabbit as though he would not get any more food for a long time. He tried to push himself up but faltered. He looked sheepishly at the other men who seemed not to pay attention to his shortcomings. With a more resolute effort, he got up from the floor, sweating from the process. He smoothed his coat with his big hands. He eyed Jeff and his family and mumbled, "It's hot in here. Ah want you to know, Masta Jeff, that ah'm gonna speak my mind. You can suspect that anyone who does not have the courage to attend this here rally would be in danger from his own people anyway. Ma'm, I didn't mean to frighten you," Randolf, said speaking to Mandy, who nodded her head sympathetically. "Ah thank you for your kind hospitality."

The men soon left. Jeff sighed, knowing he and his family would soon begin the day's labors with the Franklins.

In the pre-dawn darkness, Randolf, Jasper and the two other men stayed hidden in the woods located on the far side of town. They waited patiently for an all-clear signal. Randolf looked at his watch, trying to make out the time.

"You know, son, ah hope you believe as ah do that the hard times won't continue for everyone much longer," he said to Jasper. "Ah'm go'in to convince all the citizens that my ideas will move the area forward. Don't you think it's a good thing to move forward? Between you and me, ah heard a white say that a long time ago. Sometime you'll have to come along with me and hear more. Don't you think?" Jasper did not answer. He was too smitten by Randolf's every word even though he did not comprehend everything he said. Jasper felt the big man was free. He wondered what he should think about "moving forward?"

The politician knew that politics was all just a speculation. He said, "You see, son, politics is a roulette wheel, and move'n forward is a gamble, 'cause you don't know what you'll run into. The excitement of it all, and the fact that there be high stakes. It's important to keep the ideas flowing, develop plans all the time, and fire creativity. When you agree with me, ah'll be glad to welcome you to the fold."

Enthralled by every move and word of the politician, Jasper found all he could do was watch him with a keen eye and smile, and wish for something exciting in his life or say, "Yes, suh!" No one talked to him like that before.

He observed Randolf lowering the bushy pine needle branches to marvel at the sun's early glow. The woods awakened to the sound of birds. The smaller animals began scurrying for food. The air smelled fresh and new and spicy, like nutmeg and cinnamon ground to perfection. The men rubbed their eyes and stretched their bodies aching from many hours in the saddle.

Randolph saw Jasper paying attention, and the politician said, "Remember, son, we saw it first, and that's what ah want to be is first. It's mah aim."

No one seemed outwardly nervous while waiting for the signal. They knew it would come soon. Randolf stopped talking and hummed a soft, gentle tune. The sun's rays felt warm as they shone through the branches on the riders arms while they advanced through the forest openings and the morning dew. The men were hidden by the tall pine tree branches growing everywhere in the forest. Its stillness made the minutes go slower. No breeze echoed a sound. At last, when no one suspected it, the signal came, and the small party rode out into the sunlit opening, galloping down the red-dirt road past some of the town's buildings.

Jasper stood alone. "Whoa, boy. That freedom sure does look good. Whoa, boy. We can't go just yet. One day we'll go forward," he said to his impatient horse.

The temptation to ride with the men and board the train was difficult to resist and all Jasper could handle. He grabbed the reins tighter. He knew his father's words to be true and decided not to yield.

"Whoa, boy. Steady, boy. If we goes, there's just so many excuses my daddy could make to the Franklins. Ol Jeff would be in trouble. But look at them, boy, they goin' farther and farther away. Can barely see their stride now. Best we turn around now. Someday!"

Jasper studied the landscape ahead of him and saw no one.

A small building on the first floor housed Jim Benet's law office. The attorney slept in a big brown chair. He had been working on a case all night and dozed off. A notebook of papers, strewn across his desk, lay still and dead in the early morning light. The window was open slightly. The noises of riders and the hoof beats of the horses that suddenly passed through jarred him from his sleep.

"What the...?" he said opening his eyes as every book on the shelf seemed to move before him. Jim gripped the arm of the chair and tried to regain composure; then he dashed to the window and pulled back the curtains facing the peaceful main street.

On the corner of the street where some men were standing, stood the small red brick Bank Building. It housed the bank itself and the drugstore entrance a few feet away. The drug store had the biggest sign advertising its name right in front of its door, "Cokesbury Drug Store, W. R. Norwood, Druggist and Chemist." Next to it was a dry goods store stacked with wares everywhere. Then a building which housed the newspaper, the Abbeville Banner, seemed deserted except for one man who appeared to be working. At that moment, much to Jim's surprise, he saw some familiar faces. "What do you know? There's Tom, James and Judah across the street. They couldn't make it to the council meeting for the railroad which Greenwood got, but they made it at this early hour. Guess this shows me. I need to study personalities more."

Jim watched Tom walk among the spectators. He shook hands with a few of the men and stopped to converse with them. Jim had not come face-to-face with Tom since last month's meeting at Sam's. Jim noticed the men huddled together, conversing with each other as Tom strolled away.

"They surely are up to something. I wonder what they are saying?" said Jim quietly, as he opened the window more and stepped behind the curtain, not sure if he had been seen by anyone or not. *Could they be plotting some kind of mischief?* he wondered.

Curiosity got the better of him and he continued to observe the men. Judah and James walked together. James had a graceful stride in spite of his 6' height. He pulled something out of his pocket. *What could that be?* thought Jim. *Maybe he's checking the time.* James stood still for a minute, and Jim noticed his clothing. James had on a dark suit with a white pearl-buttoned shirt and high collar, secured with a large, black-bow tie. In the early cool morning, his long, gold buttoned overcoat put him in style.

"I wish I could have had better clothes of my own. Must be James' tailor," said Jim aloud. He thought of his home in Scotland, where he froze in the winter, since he was too poor to afford a lot of heavy clothing. Sam and Frank became his friends and gave him their cast-offs. Gifts he graciously accepted for their warmth.

Without warning, Jim became aware of utter silence on the street. James walked to his horse. The lawyer wondered if the rumors that circulated about James were true. Former soldiers said he sat out the war, making up clever plans for others to follow. He came home without a scratch, physically or mentally. Jim still had a gut feeling the rumors were true.

Judah's impatience probably got the better of him. He strolled toward the men Tom spoke to. He waved his hat and seemed to say to someone up the street, "Let's hurry. It's getting near the time."

Jim knew Judah was a young man of various means. He helped Jim obtain the teaching job at Cokesbury College when he first came to the region. Judah's family once owned a considerable amount of land, which he and his father disposed of in a gambling game. With his dark looks and agile, slender body, he easily concealed himself closer to buildings and slowly crept ahead. The rumors that spread around town said he led a couple of successful raids on the Northern camps.

His single unique distinction was his heavy, thick, dark beard, the first characteristic anyone noticed about him. Children would tease him when they saw him coming and called him "Blacky." Anger shone in his tiny beady eyes.

"I wonder who Judah is waiting for?" said Jim, bewildered. Seconds later Sam meandered onto the scene rather unimpressively, as though he was tired. He did not acknowledge Judah's greeting. He whispered something to Sam, who seemed to pay attention to Judah's words.

Sam's debonair ways and handsome features had changed

through the years. Only when the mood struck him at precisely the right moment did his old self appear with all his charm and wit. Jim knew that the company Sam kept made a difference in his personality. Sam's best moments were rare as the years passed. He remained a wounded Confederate veteran whose friends and family saw him turn sullen and temperamental.

The former soldier was heavier and getting bald. His bloodshot eyes and his forehead knitted in a frown. Jim believed he still cared for Lottie as he knew he once did. Sam made a life for her in the best way he could. At least at town gatherings, she seemed in good spirits. Some people hoped her goodness would rub off on her husband.

Sam dabbled in a number of things. He ran a store on the edge of town, talked politics with the influential council, and said the railroad idea interested him at one time. Because his late parents had the admiration of the town's people, along with his lovely wife, he remained lucky enough to command and receive the esteem of the town's citizens. They accepted the fact of his bravery in battle and pitied his left arm amputation. People never forgot his parents' kindness of food and medicine they confiscated during the war.

Jim thought of the story many older folks related to him about Sam's amputation. His companions carried him to an old church as the battle continued and the doctor examined him and said, "Sam, you've got two bullets in that arm plus a deep bullet scrape. I can't save it. We've got to remove it now."

Sam was teary eyed and delirious but he said, "Doc, you've got to let me go back in battle. I've got to get the men who shot me...I've got to fight...I've got to fight."

"Yes, Sam, you've got to fight for your life," said the doctor. "God, I wish I had better medicine!" The doctor looked at his assistants and said, "Hold him down tight!"

As far as anesthetic went, the surgeon knew there would be hardly any left to last through Sam's amputation. The story is told that Sam screamed so loud, the Union Army stopped the war for a few moments.

The townspeople loved his fighting spirit, but how true the story could be, Jim didn't know. He continued to watch the action on the street with intense interest. There appeared a man with a long white beard, but not old, wearing a long, black coat with black boots shouting, "Bring the horses near the station. Hurry!"

Jim tried to figure out what he meant. He observed more men standing around the building either talking, pacing back and forth or waiting for something to happen. Jim said, "Hmmm, I don't recall seeing these men in town. Guess I've been too busy to notice many events and circumstances."

He waited a few minutes. Men would come and go and soon Jim's irritation surfaced and he said, "If Sam remains on the street, I'm going out to see him and just talk. I sure would like to find out what plans he has for the future of this town. If he says it's not important, it's secretive. Now where did I put my coat?"

Jim checked all around the room and found it behind his desk. He grabbed it and ran out the door. Once outside, he looked in every direction and could not see one sign of Sam. Where did he disappear to so fast? Jim wondered.

Disappointed, Jim started to walk home in the opposite direction of Sam and his party. He happened to turn around

31

and saw Sam who was not in calling distance. Then he saw him vanish along a side street heading in the direction of the train.

*   *   *   *   *

"Lucky for us nobody throws things. Times must be changin'," declared Randolf to his companions as they rode out of town to the Cokesbury train station where he hoped a lot of people would be waiting. His friends laughed and said, "Lets keep a' goin'." The three men did not stop along the way. They kept their horses galloping. When Randolf and his party arrived at the depot, the politician smiled in delight.

"Hey, Ah can't believe this. See, didn't ah tell you the mah people would be here. We's going places. Hey, there," he said, jumping off his horse, pouncing to the ground and grasping the first hand he saw.

Right in front of him he saw the smiling faces of his own people in the area. He had met them at their churches before. They reached out to grab his hand and wish him well. The other two men took the horses off to the side, and silently watched the politician have his day. When they saw the turnout of people, they quietly rode away down another dirt road.

"Hurrah! Hurrah!" the crowd shouted and clapped. The women, dressed in plain clothes of gray and blue and even black and some in red, carried parasols sweeping their bodies back and forth to show off the small umbrella. Most of the men wore their work clothes and a few wore ties. They held their calloused hands into the air, waving them before the politician to touch. They were really the people Randolf wanted to reach, for other hands he shook belonged to house servants, for those hands remained smooth and toil free.

Some of the children had shoes too big for them and twirled in their plain clothes as they danced to the rhythmic clap of the crowd. One child struggled to tie her shoes and finally gave up, dancing without them.

"Ah'll get to you and you. Ah promises to shake everyone's hand," said Randolf, shouting and pointing to each constituent. While reaching for each hand, including those of the little ones, he noticed their large brown eyes fixed on the wonderment of all the excitement.

Randolf was so pleased at the turnout, he did not look down the road toward town. He kept saying, "Good you're here." "Got some special news for you." "Sisters and Brothers this is wonderful."

In time, after Randolf was sure he had greeted everyone who came to the rally, he made his way to the train platform. He went up the steps to board it, and shouts of joy came from the crowd. One man called out, "Whether you makes it or not, Brother, we's all with you."

Randolf shouted back, "Ah intends to." He pointed at the throng. "You is with me."

"Hallelujah!" the people shouted. They clapped and cheered. "Hallelujah!"

The crowd hushed, and Randolf, raising his hands for silence, spoke out as loud as he could, telling the crowd, "Ah'll be back! You jus' sit tight till then!"

He felt secure and warm in the feeling they conveyed to him by giving him their utmost attention and thought. He never felt any electricity like this before coming from a crowd. It was eerie and wonderful at the same time. It was hard to describe; it was heavenly.

I can do anything, anything ah want to. They love me, they love me. Ah wants to make them happy. They's good folks, good folks, he thought.

The train would pull out shortly, taking him to Columbia first. He dearly hoped to meet more people whom his travel companions would round up for him. He had special words for these people and a hope for their future. He thought, *the first thing I want to do is bring these friends nearer to me.* He called them closer to the train platform, like Moses, saying, "Come in so's you can hear me. Come on in." He motioned to them with his hands. When all quieted down, he spoke.

"This is a great day. It's a great day for change'n and we's goin' to change the fact that we's not supposed to be here, but, I'm goin' to change your life."

Everybody called out "Hurrah, keep on, keep a' goin'." Some danced and waved their hands in jubilation. When the spectators quieted down again, Randolf continued.

"Ah plan to see that all o' you gets a piece of what's comin' to you. We plans to get land and divide it for you. We knows we can. There's a plenty for all. We's goin' places. It's goin' to change your life."

Applause and shouts of joy permeated the small station. Hands waved and clapped.

"Hallelujah! Praise Jesus!" Many in the crowd repeated "Hallelujah!"

"Ah plans on your support. Will you all here support me?" said Randolph.

The biggest cheer went up from the crowd. "Praise Jesus, we's with you." The men shouted the loudest and clapped their hands. "Tell us how. Tell us how. Yea, hallelujah. Tell us!"

Again, this demonstration told him he was right where he needed to be. These people wanted him. It felt good inside. He made shouts of joy himself: "Bless you."

At that moment, Randolf and the people around him thought they were the only ones who existed. When the reality finally struck Randolf, realized that he was really alone amongst a small group of people. Randolf stopped talking and motioned for the engineer to start the train.

The whistle blew and startled the crowd. "Ahhhhh… Ohhhh" the crowd yelled. Then two shots rang out. One of the shots hit Randolf, and he immediately slumped over the railing, dead. Women screamed and ran.

Men shouted, "Who did this, who did this?" They scrambled every which way, looking for the person who fired the shot.

The oldest girls grabbed the littlest children and ran in every direction, looking for a safe haven. Most of the children screamed, "Mama! Mama!" The smallest children could not keep up with their older sisters and brothers. They fell and cried louder.

One boy about 10 years old begged his little sister who had fallen and scraped her knee to get up. "Come on, Yolanda. We's got to go. Peoples is comin' for us. Come on get up. Dat's better, hurry. I fixes your hurt when we get home. Hurry." He took her by both arms and ran as fast as he could, meeting their mother, who swept the child up in her arms and ran toward a store house where wood was kept.

Many older people who could not run fast enough had to fend for themselves. Some of them cried to their friends, "Wait for me! Wait for me!"

One old woman tripped over her cane. She cried, "Oh,

Lord! Don't leave me here! Don't leave me here!"

"Let's get out of here into the shed over there," an old man said who helped her up. "Quick! We've got to go."

The younger, more agile crowd of teenage girls and women split up and ran away into the woods or down the road yelling, "Help! Help!"

Some of the older people tried to keep up with the others, but it was impossible. They hid behind anything they could find, like boxes and barrels.

Men yelled, "Take the young away in the woods. Take'um away!"

A few of the farmers ran in the direction where the shots had been fired and picked up pieces of wood or anything they could find to defend themselves, if they had to from an unseen, unknown enemy. The other men followed. Randolf was still slumped over the railing on the platform. The conductor staring at his lifeless body. The shouts of joy and praises of excitement were long gone.

"Tighten our line!" said one man to the others. "We needs to be together and have our right to assemble and fight for the new ideas that Randolf said."

"Look!" screamed an older man who saw the sheriff and his party riding fast toward them. "They wants to break us up."

The 30 men who linked their arms together braced themselves. Someone in line cried out, "Anybody got a gun?"

The militia on horseback led by the sheriff, Tom, and Sam had weapons and shot into the air as they approached the group of former slaves who by law were not to congregate.

No sooner had this been said when a small band of white men appeared in the distance. Then suddenly, like a flurry of snow, the sheriff's militia arrested the black men before any could escape. One lone man tried to shout the names of the men who came toward him, but his words like the train whistle evaporated into silence. Another shouted before he was struck in the head, "We's ain't got a chance."

CHAPTER 3

Sam knelt before Lottie in the sparse living room of Tom's house. The square, nearly empty room, offered little comforts: a small sofa, a chair, and a table with candles near a window with a view of a barren field stretching for miles. Sam clutched Lottie's skirt with his right hand while burying his face in its folds like a child hiding from punishment. With her arms around him, Lottie attempted to calm his shaking body. Tom's widow, Etta, sobbed in the next room while the wooden casket boards were nailed together.

Sam looked up at his wife with her blond curls neatly settled around her head, the sweet angelic face, blue eyes, and soft pink cheeks that kept her youthful looking to him. "Why did this have to happen?" he cried in dismay. "Why did Tom have to die? Everything was planned down to the last detail. Tom and I would get the money when we got to the cabin in North Carolina, Lottie. We'd pay the debt on the land there. It would be ours. We'd leave pain and punishment behind forever." He stopped for a second. "Since the politician was shot, people have been suspicious of the volunteer militia I took part in, but they were only doing their duty. Blacks can't gather in a group like they did at the station."

"Sam, there's been all kinds of rumors about the incident I don't understand. We'll leave soon if you want. Don't you think we should lay Tom to rest first?"

"Yes. I can't ever replace what was blown away. With one arm I can't even build you a house…I can't. That's why this was all so perfect, but Tom died."

"I know. You miss Tom. He was really more than kin to you, more than a friend."

Sam tightened his grip on her skirts and said, "We could accomplish anything, Lottie, once we set our minds to it. Together we had control. Tom helped me keep it too, even to the point of making sure the railroad was not begun here until we said it could start."

Lottie stood up and Sam let go of his grip. She walked to the chair and sat down.

"Sam, isn't there too much talk of the railroad coming?"

Sam gritted his teeth and said, "Lottie, it's not coming here. The area is not ready. The community needs to grow more to support it. Tom and I had a plan concerning the railroad. It played out well for a time until the outside interference came, and that's been stopped."

"You mean, Jim. I thought you settled that business with Frank and Jim at the meeting at our house."

"Nothing was settled. Just talk and more talk in the wrong direction, and Jim leaving in a huff. Tom's dead! People will think I had something to do with it."

"Nonsense! How could you?"

"We were alone on the road in the wagon. He keeled over, didn't speak a word. I shook him a little…he didn't revive. He fell over."

"Sam, if that's what happened, then that's what happened. You and I…his family…we know Tom wasn't well."

"That's not it. We were alone. We argued just like before. It's nothing unusual. At times though other people heard us. They may say or do things…think things that are not true."

"Sam, who? Who will say or do what?"

Before he could answer, Lottie put her fingers over his mouth. They both listened and heard Tom's widow sobbing harder in the next room. They peered out the door and saw that the casket Tom's sons built appeared ready to receive the body.

"I better help," said Sam.

Lottie waited in silence. She was aware that only a few days had passed since the shooting incident at the train. She listened in silence while waiting on the customers in the store who gossiped about the disturbance.

"Say, did ya see how that one black fella fought?" said the first man.

"Sure did. Till the sheriff come by and hit him and he fell over," said the second man.

"Please, Mister Tift," said a woman customer. "I don't want to hear anymore."

When the woman left the store, the first man continued. "Yes, sir, many men were involved. Confusion existed everywhere. Someone fired the fatal shot. I don't know who, do you?"

The customer shook his head.

Lottie's skepticism kept her from finding the truth, for there was so much talk, it was hard to separate the truth from the lies. Was Sam or Tom involved, Lottie thought? If so, how much? On the other hand, she was sure there had been no serious argument between her husband and his cousin. Nonetheless, everything that happened was all too sudden.

Lottie turned and headed to the door, only to stop a

moment and gather her thoughts. She mumbled, "Sam said there was an argument. Tom, sick for a long time, did not complain, even though his pain may have been unbearable. There were no sores or physically visible wounds to indicate foul play." She walked up and down the small room. Thoughts came to her about Sam's temper. She sat down in a chair. Details were going through her mind. Lottie got up again and paced the floor. She kept questioning herself. *Could Sam have prolonged their disagreement, which could have been too much for Tom? Yet Sam brought the body home in Tom's own wooden wagon...only the way he brought the body home.*

At the time, she remembered then that she had been assisting George Franklin and Gideon O'Neil, the Franklin nephew, when Sam motioned to her excitedly from the window and slipped away.

"Excuse me, gentlemen, I'll have to look at the stock," said Lottie, hastily heading for the door. "Moses," she said to a helper, "serve these men."

She followed Sam who kept looking behind him perhaps to make sure no one was following. When Lottie caught up with Sam, she found Tom's small wagon standing inconspicuously between two big trees.

Sam put his hand over her mouth to stifle a scream. Tom's body lay in the back of the wagon among the debris of leaves, pine needles, dark-brown liquor bottles and scraps of tin the men had found on the road.

"My heaven, I'm going to faint," she said softly. "Tom dead in all that mess!"

Sam steadied her as they quickly drove away in the wagon with Tom's body.

After they arrived at Tom's home, swift preparations continued for the burial. Lottie knew the overly-concerned citizens, really the noisy ones, would be asking what happened to Tom. Just how could the family explain? The hidden facts of land in North Carolina, Tom's hurried funeral, the drinking and gambling before his death could not be kept a secret for long. Everyone agreed that Tom had looked sickly. He complained of stomach pains, but still kept up with the things like farming, the North Carolina ventures, and gambling. He truly was unafraid and energetic just as he had been when he aided the militia the day of the riot. Some citizens on the street said it appeared as though he led the men.

Sam came in and moved over to the sofa, covering his face with his hands. After a few moments, Sam looked up. This time he was perspiring and looked pale. Lottie wiped his head with a handkerchief. He arose and supported himself on the edge of the table.

"I believe I never felt more depressed than the day my arm was cutoff. If only I could escape somewhere for awhile. There's a little money left over from the gambling I did with Tom as we headed for North Carolina. If only I could leave this place; maybe I could straighten out the situation later and relieve anyone's doubts. I could go away."

Lottie went up to her husband and tried to hold his hand, but he pulled his arm away and looked toward the door.

"Sam, don't do this to me!" she cried, becoming afraid and on the verge of tears. She bit her lip, took a deep breath, and continued. "Sam, I know this grieves you, for both you and Tom were as close as brothers, but I truly admit I'm afraid, for I must confess I'm confused. If you leave now, I'll be alone to face everyone's questions. What do I say to people who are surely bound to find out about Tom's death and become suspicious? What words can I use? How do I answer their questions?"

Lottie could hold out no longer. Tears came to her eyes, and she began to cry. Her feelings, her thoughts and all the doubts that she held inside were unbearable, and there was no choice but to release the emotion. Sam, touched by her sadness, held her close and stroked her cheek.

"There, there, now. No need for you to carry on this way. You know how tough Tom was."

He patted her on the back, and when she regained her composure, he guided her to the chair where she might be more comfortable.

"This pounding is giving me a headache! I hope they are almost finished sealing the box. We must get on to the grave site now, so people can think Tom is buried in North Carolina, and I can settle any issues there."

He looked at Lottie. Her expression showed dismay, for he knew her questions were not answered.

"Listen, my dearest, I know there may be suspicions about me, since I was the only person with Tom when he died. Simply tell the curious of his chest pain. We were riding in his wagon to North Carolina…he collapsed. Tell your friends that Tom's wishes were to be buried there. Etta can have some prayers with friends later. She doesn't want a lot of people around. Forget what other people think. We'll do our own thinking. Besides, everyone knows Tom's skin color was not good. He had lost weight and hardly ever went to a doctor. That truth alone should satisfy them. In the meantime, directly after the funeral, that is, I'll have to take care of a few details myself."

Sam wrung his hands and turned to the window to hide his face. Lottie went up to him and said, "What sort of details?"

Sam turned to her. "You know…our land in North Carolina. Let's just say railroad investments. We agreed that you want to be out of that store someday. Tom and I bought the land. He owed me the money anyway. His share is hidden in a secret place at the cabin there, and I think I know where. I'll settle the business of it and later be back. You saw no one after I picked you up at the store. Right? I saw no one either and no one has seen me since Tom and I left. Did you say anything to anyone, did you?" Her tight blonde curls scarcely moved as she shook her head. "Only you and a few others knew we were headed there, and for the time, being that's better," concluded Sam.

"Well, I don't know."

Sam perspired, and he took a handkerchief out of his pocket to pat his brow. He then replied, "It'll be a little awhile. I've got to get away till things calm down."

"Sam, think, think. Are you sure you want to do this?" Sam nodded. "If you leave now, what will happen? Besides, did someone hurt Tom because of the riot after that politician was shot?"

"No, no, Lottie. Someone got an itchy finger, maybe James or Judah. I don't know for sure. You know I can't aim well with just this arm."

"What about Tom? He didn't do it, did he?"

"No, I don't think he shot the politician. He was with me and the militia."

"Well, many people were hurt by the rioting and the shock of it all even happening."

"Look at the dreadful shock!" Sam pointed to his arm stub. "Look at the hurt."

Lottie pleaded, "Ask James or Frank to help. They have money."

"Yes, but James always demands repayment and wants to make a profit. Frank is a close friend, almost like kin. I've known him a long time. I couldn't ask him!"

"Perhaps you could inquire of Jim."

"Why should I?"

"Well, why not? Sam, you need help and someone to help you, advise you. Your family gave him help, even financial help when he first came here. He had nothing."

Sam paced the floor and turned to Lottie and said, "There are some things I would not want an attorney to know. It's… political. If Jim had not become an attorney, I might approach him, but as it stands now, it's out of the question. We don't have the same circle of friends we used to have…we have differences. We're not the kin we used to be."

"I guess those are your reasons. Although with you gone, what will Etta do?"

Sam did not answer. He walked to the door. The pounding had stopped, and he was sure it was getting near the time for them to leave. He turned to Lottie and said, "She'll manage. I'll give her something."

"Yet, you still want to inquire of James?"

"I know, dearest, but as I said, he demands repayment quickly. Nevertheless, do I sense some doubt in your mind? It will be in others,' too. Just tell them he died of a heart attack. He did!"

"Sam, I have no doubts about you."

He ran to her arms and bent to kiss her, when suddenly the door burst open and Tom's son said, "Hurry, hurry. We've got to go now."

When the couple got in Tom's small wagon for the ride to the cemetery, it was hitched to two horses. Lottie's feelings overwhelmed her again. She felt like screaming. She sensed the wagon had been marked by Tom's death and not fit to ride in. Her body shook as though she was cold, as cold as death. She gasped, "God, it's Tom's wagon." Sam put his arm around her for a second while he explained.

"We have nothing else to ride in. All the other wagons and buggies and horses are taken by the adults and children." He sensed Lottie's fears and repeated, "I already told you Tom said that he felt a severe pain and fell over. That's all, I tell you. That's all!" He grabbed the reins. The horses went forward.

"There will be no doubt or questions on these issues," she said softly. "After all, what else is there to do?"

She knew it was useless to try and bring Sam to his senses and not run away from whatever bothered him. Tom's death could not be changed. Lottie, aware that she had no more confidence in herself or Sam, decided to reply to inquiries just as Sam recommended.

She looked at her husband, but he was driving the wagon. He had to be careful, the road was rough and, of course, they had the wagon with the casket.

"Sam, I can't think now. I'm scared."

"Be discreet. Then no one will suspect a thing. I won't go far."

Tom's son, in the first wagon, took a different trail to the cemetery while the others followed. This way no one would see the funeral procession. Sam knew the country well and let his mind wander to the people who were helped by his parents in the past. He thought of some farmers now deceased and people nearby who still owed his family money from before the war. He speculated they could pay him some cash so he could stay away for awhile until he found the money Tom hid in the cabin, or wait until this situation cleared up. He could give Etta some money, pay off Tom's debts, and buy the retreat in North Carolina.

"I'll send one of the boys to get James. We'll pass near his farm on our way," Sam said.

CHAPTER 4

The four wagons and horses the children rode, moved closer together. The trail had not been used for several years, and the embedded rocks along the uneven ground, together with the roots of the lofty pines and the towering oaks caused the wagons to sway. The drivers, fearful of the wagons tipping over, slowly and carefully drove their vehicles across the pine needle trail into the shadows of the secluded forest. Eighteen relatives and close friends of Etta and Tom felt safe there.

Through time, pine straw had fallen on the road covering the way. In case anyone would remember and try to use the trail, they would have a difficulty finding it, thought Sam. He knew this was the best way to the cemetery, although no one else would ever think of going this way again. He knew that slaves passed here years before, especially the ones who were mistreated and abused. They sought refuge from their master's whip and their mistresses' abusive words to avoid a beating. When people talked about this place, they said there were ghosts here who hung from the trees and called out in deep, agonizing tones. A few curious adventurers came but always ran away, scared of their own shadows.

No one spoke on the journey, and each driver concentrated on the task which lay ahead; to bury Tom as secretly as possible. Tom's family agreed with Sam, that he could take charge of the

North Carolina property and any money he found. The quick burial would lead the citizens to think Tom was dead and buried in North Carolina. Sam looked up at the oak trees mixed in with tall pines. Each tree struggled to reach the sunlight. *The oak leaves will change their color,* thought Sam. *I won't change my mind about what I want to do. In North Carolina, my world is locked in, and everything else is locked out.*

He allowed his thoughts to wander to the people his family had helped in the past, especially those who still owed money to his late parents and had never paid their debts. *About everybody I can think of is dead because of the war and its destruction. Oh yes, the Franklins. George is such a funny fellow the way he shuffles around. Drusilla, that sister of his, drives me crazy with her no-give attitude and pinched expression.* Suddenly, his wagon would not move. *Oh, no! The wheel is stuck in some mud.*

"Hey, wait. The wagon is stuck," he shouted to the others.

He jumped out of the wagon. Lottie climbed out herself. She stood aside while he ran ahead to have the others bring their shovels. After all, he drove the wagon with the casket in the back, and the jolt had moved it. Alfred, Etta's brother, and Tom's older sons, went to look for long pieces of wood they could shove under the wheel to help loosen it. Sam watched Lottie. Her shallow, drawn face reflected her tired spirit while she greeted him with a helpless blank stare.

"Lottie, don't worry," said Sam. He was not sure that she heard him.

One of the other wagons carried Tom's widow and some relatives who walked over to stand next to her. The children who rode the other four saddled horses stopped and stayed close by the adults.

Sam reiterated to himself, *I know! I'll get James to help. He knows how to get away for awhile, and I'll somehow handle, or make him believe I'll handle, his interest charges. Unless I can think of someone I don't like and put the pressure on that person for cash. Abbeville and Greenwood are not as rich as other farming areas or as good as Frank's farm, but I can't bother him. I'll come to some conclusion shortly...maybe right after the burial. I need enough money to live and settle finances for the land and build a house in North Carolina. It might be several months before I return, or as long as it takes for any suspicions to subside.*

"Uncle Sam!" said one of his nephews. "We need help with the digging. Grab a shovel."

"Oh, I'll help," said Sam, rousing himself from his deep thoughts.

He thought as he pushed the shovel in the mud. *I can't stand facing any townspeople. They're nosy. I don't want to hear all their questions. I want to get out of here.* He dropped his shovel when the wagon was loose and let the other men finish. He stood next to Lottie and whispered, "I know of a few people in town who heard me quarrel with Tom about three days before he died." Lottie turned and stared at him.

"It was a silly argument over a horse that wandered onto Tom's farm. What bothers me is how much they really heard, especially about our gambling and whose horse had wandered away. We even talked about Tom's gambling debts."

"If they didn't stare at you, maybe they didn't hear what you and Tom said."

"That's a point, my dear. I feel the pressure inside me to get away from here. It's better if Tom's debt is paid off in North Carolina; then the land is mine. No questions asked. After all,

Tom had never grasped his responsibilities, or was willing to split the property in favor of me. With Tom gone, I know leaving the area is the best way. I don't have to explain anything."

"Then you did argue, Sam? Lord, didn't you?"

"Yes."

"I am still upset. Etta's getting nervous. I hope we'll be moving soon," said Lottie.

In no time at all, with everyone doing his part, the wagons began to move again. Lottie asked herself, *what will come out of all of this? Who will help me? I wonder if I should talk to Jim, but what would Sam say? Jim would have the answers now that he is an attorney, and maybe he could even help make the arrangements on the North Carolina land Sam and Tom claim they own. Jim assists when anyone asks him for something. He listens until you are finished talking to him. I can see how Lauren feels secure with him. He never lets her down. He takes an interest in what she does no matter how insignificant it is. She never does anything important though…poor soul, she is sickly and keeps to herself when she has dizzy spells. Anyway, Jim treats her like a queen. Once Sam had everything. I was a queen too. Now he's changed. What to do? What to do?*

To the small group, it seemed to take forever to arrive at the burial plot. Etta looked wearily at Alfred. "Aren't we coming there soon? Seems like when we pass this hill we're almost there."

Alfred shuffled in his seat and said, "This darn wagon is the most uncomfortable. Yup, we'll be there soon, just after we cross over Rocky Creek and go up the sandbank. When the trail circles and opens into a field that touches the edges of farm land, we know the valley of hills covered with oaks and pines is there. Nice place to rest."

"Why do you suppose Sam is so nervous?" said Etta, fighting back tears.

"Don't know. Don't know. Might never find that out. Sam's a peculiar man to figure out. He and Tom always had something going here or there. Probably argued over whatever it was, and Tom just gave out. Don't look good his goin' to North Carolina. I ain't leavin'. Hope you're not." Alfred looked at her sternly.

"Why should I want to go there? Why?" said Etta, with tears streaming down her face. "Tom's out of his misery. Thank God! The pain he suffered. I'm surprised he lived as long as he did."

Alfred fell silent, but mumbled under his breath, "With Sam around, anything can happen."

* * * * *

Nestled in a corner clearing near some deep woods, the mourners gathered around the hurriedly dug grave as the men quickly lowered the casket. The minister, paid to keep the burial quiet for the time being, conducted a short service. Sam only heard words which sounded like drums beating the pulse of time. Unaware of his movements, he reached for his lost arm and cursed under his breath, remembering it was gone. Then Lottie tapped his shoulder. He looked in the direction of her nod. To his surprise, he saw a couple stop their small buggy close to the wagons. The group watched in silence as the frail woman and her aging male companion headed toward them. George Franklin offered his arthritic bent fingered hand to Tom's widow and said, "Anythin' ah can do?"

Drusilla put her slender arms around Etta's waist and said,

"We're so sorry to hear of your loss. What happened to Tom? Why is he to be buried here?" There was no answer.

George made his way toward the men as a breeze took his thick, white hair and stood it on end. His colorless clothing made him appear ghostly as he approached the group. The men took him aside.

Sam stared at Drusilla. Her thin, wavy hair, pulled back in a bun, tightened her drawn face and whitish skin. Her squinty eyes appeared sharp and cunning. The long fingers of her hands were calloused from years of work. The fingers reached out to the other women, who responded coolly, but did not answer her questions. Even Sam refused to acknowledge her gesture of sympathy.

Sam grabbed Lottie's arm and whispered, "What are they doing here? Who told them? Maybe they came because they're suspicious of something they heard or saw."

"But Sam," said Lottie putting her hand over her mouth to keep her voice low, "They also knew your parents, although I don't know how they heard of Tom's death. I fear we'll have to tell Tom's friends of his death."

Sam held her arm tighter and said, "Just remember what I told you to say, except this burial will be told all over town very soon. The secrecy is ruined now. The rest I'll take care of. I dislike Drusilla's looks and self-centered ways. She has no expression on her face and her gloomy appearance makes her miserly looking."

"Shh, shh. She'll hear you. You don't want that right now."

Everyone at the grave site knew the Franklins were unappreciative people. This made them difficult to communicate with. To those who had never been acquainted with them, they seemed irreproachable and secretive, revealing little about themselves.

Sam continued to watch Drusilla and commented in low tones, "I'll always dislike her looks; most of all, I loathe her readiness to grab whatever she can grab with her bony fingers."

The minister made another announcement for the family, but Sam still had difficulty concentrating and looked at the distant trees. His eyes wandered to the far point of the path where he caught a glimpse of three men steadily approaching on horseback.

"Lottie!" said Sam whispering in her ear. "Look who's coming. I don't want them to see me."

"What? Who?" said Lottie, looking around.

The others saw the riders too and slowly edged themselves to the thick cluster of trees near the cemetery's edge. Sam kissed his wife and rode off into the forest.

When the three men arrived in the midst of the small assemblage, the mourners recognized the sheriff and his deputies. They walked and sang, "The Lord is good. He giveth and taketh."

They continued singing while the deputies remained on horseback, but the tall, muscular sheriff, J. F. C. DuPre dismounted and handed the reins to a deputy. He straightened his hat and took long strides while fingering his holster. When he stood before the widow, he studied each person present. Everyone stood silently waiting for him to speak.

"Mighty sorry, ma'am. What happened? My deputy spotted your wagons aways back. He says it looks like you carried a wooden box."

"Sheriff, Tom's been awful sick. Awful sick," sobbed Etta.

"Me and the boys are truly sorry. We saw Tom at the store not too long ago. He looked in good spirits but tired. What did he catch? Smallpox or something?"

No one made a sound. They waited for Etta to answer. DuPre looked at Lottie and asked, "Where's Sam?"

Lottie could not answer. She hoped Etta would think of something to say about Tom. Instead, Lottie lunged forward putting her arms around Etta, who started to cry uncontrollably. Lottie covered Etta with her shawl and attempted to calm her while leading her to the wagon.

"She needs to get home," one of the older boys said.

"Get Etta into the wagon," another young man said.

DuPre and his deputies followed close behind. "Miss," said DuPre, tapping one of the women on the shoulder. "I just want to ask a couple of questions. We're all taken back with this happenin'."

The woman turned around and said, "Tom was sick, awful sick." Another woman repeated her statement.

One of Sam's nieces, an eight-year-old with big blue eyes and red hair, stared at the sheriff. She was the last to get on her horse.

"Why, Miss. You're an attractive miss. Can you tell me if Sam was here? Did you see him?"

She answered, "Yes, sir."

"Do you know where he went?"

Her mother came from behind. "We best go now…it's getting late. Say goodbye to the sheriff."

She yanked the girl away as the sheriff saw which direction she pointed.

CHAPTER 5

A small, rickety buggy bounced along the uneven rocky road heading in the direction of Indigo Springs. The old mare pulling the buggy traveled this ground many times, and she knew exactly where to step. The horse knew just where the twists and turns existed as though she had memorized them. Neither of the buggy's two passengers spoke to each other but stared at the scenery as they passed all the landmarks of each tree and bush along the road. In the distance, a few squirrels jumped across the road, and George mumbled, "Ah wish ah had my rifle." But his passenger paid no attention to her brother's rambling.

Late in the afternoon, the air turned cooler, and the woman huddled in the blanket, tucking it around herself. The leaves fell from the maple trees, but Drusilla failed to notice them; her mind was occupied by thoughts of Tom's funeral together with the cool reception she had felt from Tom's family. Finally, Drusilla broke the silence and addressed her brother. She cleared her throat to get his attention and looked at him.

"The reception to us was cold after we drove all that way out of Indigo Springs in respect for Tom. They seemed not to recognize me and acted like I was some distant relative not heard from in a long time. To think I used to do things for them way back in better times. One sure forgets! The only person half-way courteous was Lottie and even she seemed nervous. I 'spect it's only 'cause you go to that store and buy."

She pulled the blanket up to her neck and waited for a reply, but there was none.

George looked straight ahead. His mind was on other things.

"You know you don't shop much. We got the money, we oughta spend a bit more. Any store wants to sell. I just bought me something there," said George.

"Wasted money, no doubt, like you always do," said Drusilla.

"Now ya know I always tells you everything that goes on. Ya pretend you don't care, but I knows you listens. I knows," said George.

"Well, I know one thing. People aren't like they used to be greetin' you and askin' polite questions. Now, they're unkind and less generous. I made up my mind that it's better to stay like we are in our own seclusion than be with a bunch of nosy visitors wantin' to know what you do and do not possess," said Drusilla.

George cracked the whip over the horse, and the animal trotted faster, eyeing the path straight ahead.

"We attended that funeral out of respect," added Drusilla. "No one can say we didn't 'cause we knew the original family. It was the right thing to do. Just think, if it hadn't been for Gideon telling us of Tom's son asking him for long nails for a wooden box, we would never have known. Sure noticed, there weren't many people there."

Drusilla stopped talking. She could see her brother twitch his mouth, ready to say something.

"Woman, you keep your eyes open, you hear? 'Spect they'll

be tendin' to some business. The boys tole me ta keep quiet about all I seen. Ain't seen nothin' but a grave! Don't know rightly what he died of," said George.

"Nobody does. He sure was sick, folks say," said Drusilla.

"They thinks they gotta hold on me 'cause word got out 'bout that shootin' at the ol train depot," said George.

"You weren't there! Who told you? Seems like to me there was lots o' folks there watchin' from behind doors," replied Drusilla.

"Gideon tole me. He heard from somebody else. Don't know who. Ain't important," said George as he cracked the whip at the horse once more.

The couple rode past Frank Fuller's prosperous farm. No one was in sight. Deep in their hearts, they envied the veteran's large piece of rich land and the succession of crops it produced. Sadly, George remembered what had happened on that farm before the war.

"Can't get that nasty Miz Fuller out of my mind," said George. "She was mean ta me after all I done for her. She let me plant the seed that would bring forth the indigo, the blue dye, so's I could start the fad for the ladies of the community an' make pretty colored dresses. I know'd it woulda put Indigo Springs on the map. We wouldn't be watchin' every penny today, no sir!"

George knew that Mrs. Fuller had knowledge of others near the coast who raised the indigo years ago. The juice was extracted from the leaves and stems when they were at their fullest.

"My, it was pretty," George exclaimed. "We put it in a large vat to cure, and when it was cured, I knew it."

Drusilla didn't say a word, but let George talk. He told the story of the blue dye to anyone who would listen. This angered her, for she felt it was no one's business.

"When she 'spected I had a few orders for the indigo and was a'gettin more, she raised the price o' the land higher so's I couldn't pay. She wouldn't listen." His voice cracked. "I begged and pleaded with her for more time, but she just said no. To this day, I hate to see that place. I know somewhere we had the money to pay!"

"George, we did not have the money," said Drusilla. "If it were now, for we saved and saved, we could pay her, but she's dead. It's no use cryin. It's gone. But you gotta thank Mrs. Turner, bless her soul. She was the kindest person on this earth!"

"Ya, she was the kindest given me that money ta cover those expenses. She died 'fore I could pay her back."

"In fact, no one has ever asked for it," said Drusilla curtly.

"I hope it never comes up, but things have a strange way of turnin'," said George.

"How much money do you suppose Mrs. Fuller made all that time?"

"Ha, ha. Plenty. She destroyed the crop. Her slaves made sure there was no trace anywhere, so's no one would get credit," said George.

The couple rode home in silence. This was the most they had talked in a long time, thought Drusilla.

* * * * *

After covering the plate of biscuits in the Franklin cabin, Jeff's wife breathed a sigh of relief and exclaimed, "Massa

59

George and Miz Drusilla is gone. What a blessin'. I'm tired. I'm tired." She felt free from a burden when the Franklins were gone for awhile. They found more for her to do when they were around. Her back ached too like Jeff's. She sat down in Drusilla's kitchen chair. It had big, crumpled pillows on it whose creases fit into her aching back. It felt good. She closed her eyes and opened them for fear of dozing off to sleep. She jumped up and glanced out the little window and noted the position of the sun above the trees. "Lord, don't lets me sleep else Miz Drusilla catch me." Finished with her tasks, Mandy closed the door and called to her husband.

"Ah'm going to the cabin. Ah's finished with da chores."

Jeff nodded, put the tools away, and intended to follow Mandy but glanced around the premises. He always experienced a painful uneasiness until the Franklins returned.

"Ah wish they'd be home by now. Ah gets scared and worried. Oh, me!" Jeff mumbled to himself. "Miz Drusilla don't tell us where she's a'goin' at anytime, but Massa George he always mentions a name, except for today."

Jeff scuffed across the road and hesitated when he felt the aches and pains again.

The landscape of the Franklins showed up a dull color and empty looking in late October. Jeff wished for spring. The dogwood trees and azaleas would bloom a very beautiful pink and white, and the yellow jasmine would fill the air with sweetness. Jeff's nose twitched as he pretended to smell the blossoms. He walked down his path and up over the slope to where the heaping sand pile hid his figure. He glanced at the cabin whenever he felt the inclination and watched for any activity that might occur there.

"Hmmm. They's still not back. Wonder if they gone to their nephews, or with one o' their relatives, or maybe one o' the church members. Darned if I knows," grumbled Jeff.

The former slave looked toward the field, for once while working during the afternoon, he thought he heard a horse whinny. It could have been Doc Waddell's old mare. She sometimes strayed. Anyway, at the time, Jeff's mind was too preoccupied to pay attention to the situation.

He stopped. He did not make a sound or move. It occurred to him that something was moving in the bushes several feet from his employer's cabin. He listened intently for a moment and saw a big jackrabbit turn and follow the narrow horse's trail far to the right of the homespun cabin. Then it hopped into the field and the broad wooded covering.

"My, my. That be the biggest one I ever did see. Ah got to get me Massa Georges's rifle now."

Not many game animals were close by except rabbits and squirrels, and the old man decided to retrieve George's rifle and chase the rabbit.

Jeff hobbled as fast as he could across the sandbank and into the Franklin cabin. He knew this would break all the rules, but he needed the rifle to shoot the game. He was too tired to lure the rabbit into a trap. He checked the ammunition and hurried out the door.

His pains were gone momentarily as he thought of nothing but good, hot, rabbit stew, which he would gladly share with his employers, since he deviously confiscated the rifle for a moment of glory. He stopped short for a minute in order to catch his breath, and in a great air of anticipation rushed to seek his game.

Excited at the prospect of hot stew and killing an animal on his own, Jeff circled the area where no breeze would give his scent away. The big fat rabbit rested and sat calmly near an old fallen fruit tree. Jeff took aim. He mumbled under his breath, "Ah got you." He felt the spirit of exhilaration flow through him as he held the rifle.

* * * * *

In a few moments the horse and carriage stopped at the Franklin's door. Drusilla descended without waiting for her brother. She ruffled her skirts and hurriedly folded the blanket that had kept her warm on the trip home. She disappeared into the cabin. George removed the harness and led the animal to the pasture behind the dwelling. Just as soon as he rounded the corner of the cabin again, he was accosted by a well-dressed figure.

"Why'er you sneakin' aroun' this way?" demanded George as he backed away from the impressive-looking man, whose appearance disturbed him.

"Waitin' for you, George," said James. "I was sent by a friend o' yours whose mother lent you money a long time ago. You know how it is; your friend could use it now. I think he said he'd take $300 of what was owed 'em, and he'd forget the rest. I'll wait here. You go get it," said James, his hands gripping his holster.

"No, no, James. Ah owed his mama. She died. Ah don't owe Sam nothin'."

"Now jus' a minute ol fella. Don't pass up a good deal."

"Ah ain't your ol fella."

"You know what I'm talk'n about...the money you owed Miz Turner. Go get it."

"Ah knows, but I want no quarrel. Ah got no money an' barely make it here. Ya kin see that compared to all the others."

James leaned toward George, but Drusilla heard them talking and came out of the cabin with a big stick.

"Git outta here," she muttered threatening James with the stick.

James backed off cautiously. He held out his hands in case he had to defend himself against this frail woman who he suspected had a strong swing. He was a few feet away and hurried to his horse tied up in the woods. A shot rang out, and a few birds in the tall oak trees fluttered away. George and Drusilla ducked into the cabin.

Jeff trudged a few feet with his prize and sat down on a tree stump. He examined the rabbit and breathed heavily, thankful to have shot the animal. He retrieved his knife and began skinning the critter before darkness set in. At that moment, he listened and heard the sound of a large four-legged animal on the thick pine needles, going as fast as he could through the thicket.

"Oh, Lord be praised! What did yo' send me now?"

He decided to be out of sight. He picked up the half-skinned rabbit and headed for the thicket to reload the rifle in case he needed it again. Jeff crouched down.

"Now wouldn't it be silly," he chuckled to himself, "if it happened to be Doc Waddell's mare. It musta be only a few feet away."

He looked up and out through the entangled brush, careful not to make or show any signs of his being there. Jeff was surprised to see a rider of considerable height instead of a doe or buck. From the rear, it was difficult to detect any identification, but just as Jeff concentrated on the rider, his hands shook and his stomach pains returned. The old man moaned in discomfort and tried to forget his aches by thinking about the tall man. Who could it be? Jeff only saw his back.

After a few minutes, Jeff came out into the open. He thought the man rode off in a great hurry. Maybe he came through these parts when he heard the gunshot.

"Hmmm, maybe it's Captain Fuller, a fine man, always polite. No, he never comes calling. At least, never since the indigo argument years ago. Maybe it was Massa Turner, he came once a long time ago, but this man had arms. Just maybe the rider was Captain King. Yes, it looked like him. He rides tall and straight and showy. Whoever it was, ah ain't never gonna ask ol George. Massa don't talk much 'bout any visitors. The rider's no never mind anyway."

He sniffed the air. "Guess that smell of game is gettin' to me. Ah sure do want that rabbit dinner."

Soon the smell overpowered him so much that he forgot his trend of thought and hurried home. On the way, the discomfort returned, and he felt it hard and heavy, just like the night Randolf and his party slipped into his cabin. He knew too that he was bound to explain to Massa George and Miz Drusilla about the rifle, but he also was aware that as soon as they saw the rabbit his wife would be cooking for dinner, everything would be all right. He tapped at the cabin door and called, "Massa George and Miz Drusilla. Ah's got a big dinner for you that Mandy's gonna cook. Massa George and Miz Drusilla!"

The door opened just enough for someone to peer out.

CHAPTER 6

November brought days of cooler weather to the area. This was the time when the men in the community, who were either friends or enemies, would display their best shots in the sport of hunting opossum, raccoon, and wild turkey, even deer, if they saw one. When that ostentatious display of skill wore off, one of the prominent land owners of Cokesbury, and a keeper of fox hounds, would gather everyone who owned a horse from far and near for a hunt on his vast plantation. There happened to be more men ready to hunt than at any other season. Those without horses and preferred to walk, were allowed to shoot game in the west field. Large and small groups of men gathered in the land owner's vast field. The well-to-do men wore their best jackets, while others, not affording such luxury, wore anything they had. The men shook hands with old friends and greeted new acquaintances. The arrivals paraded their horses and wagons and parked their wagons near a wooden fence and gaped at the commotion around them as many talked, laughed, argued about the hunt, and opened their whiskey containers to satisfy their thirst. Many tested their rifles or loaded them in readiness. Some men dressed warm, others did not have the means to change their wardrobe, and some men were too poor to worry about appearances.

Jim led his horse through the field passed a group of men

and smiled at each one and shook hands. Friends came up to ask him questions and he responded. "Thanks, I'm feeling fine," he answered to someone who called out to him. "Yes, I love this excitement. I'm ready. I'm ready!" he shouted. "Never got a chance to do this in Scotland. The sport was always for the rich, you know." A small contingent of men laughed with him.

Some men gaped at the commotion around them as many talked, laughed, argued about the hunt, and opened their whiskey containers to satisfy their thirst. Many tested their rifles or loaded them in readiness. Some men were dressed warm, others did not have the means to change their wardrobe, and some men were too poor to worry about appearances.

Jay Watkins, an old-time farmer of the community and known to all by his last name, cornered Jim as he passed through the crowd of men with his horse. "Say Jim, did ya ever shoot a fox?" The old man's white beard was long and thick, covering his small face. His nose stuck out through the thickness like a small pimple, and his lips barely moved when he talked.

This caused Jim to listen carefully and say, "No, old friend, I never have. I'm really looking forward to it. Tell me, have you?"

"Right so! It was after the war. Things was scarce."

"Yes, I know, but what happened?" Jim knew he could not leave without asking.

"It was early morning. I 'member the sun was slowly come'n aroun' to sayin' good morning to the world. Heard a scratchin' sound. Didn't pay no attention 'cause sometimes there's all sorts of noises. I went into the henhouse to roun' up a few eggs laid by Annie, one o' my prize hens one of the Yankees didn't get. It was quiet. I could hardly hear a peep. Nor a cluck! Wondered what was wrong."

He stopped and rubbed his beard.

"Go on," said Jim, interested.

"In that little henhouse, wouldn't you know it? There he was a sittin' and lickin' his chops right there in Annie's nest."

"The fox. What did you do, sir?" inquired Jim.

"Betcha I didn't have my gun. Right disgusting! 'Twas in the house. I closed the door o' the henhouse, and it was only me and ol' Reynard. He didn't like it much. Made every attempt to try an' escape by the small hole he squeezed through in the first place. I found it an' covered it up with some boards I had layin' around. He ran skiddle-de-romp under every nest in there."

"Jay, I'll bet you had a time catching the ol' boy," answered Jim who hoped he could move on through the crowd.

"Yes, sir. Chased him with a burlap bag of feed I found. We ran around that little house with speed."

"I have to ask, did you catch the fox?"

"Yup! You wanta know what I did with him? He was a fighter. You see the tail on my cap?"

"Watkins, you are amazing," said Jim as he looked at his fox-tail hat. "I hope I can tell you my story after today." He patted Watkins on the shoulder as he made his way through the crowd.

"Jim," shouted Frank. "Good to see you. Tie your horse over there till hunt time. I stopped at your office several days ago, but you were not there. Your place sure is nice."

"I may have been out on a case. It has been busy for me lately."

"I've so much to talk about with you. Let's step over here. I want you to meet some men from Greenville. One of them is a relative of John C. Calhoun, our former congressmen. These men brought their special rifles. I guess these rifles are the newest equipment on the market."

While Jim and Frank talked to the men with rifles, another group of hunters brought their sons for the first time. The young men could join the hunt if they could ride their horses to chase the fox, but not necessarily shoot. Otherwise, with no horse to ride, the boys could try their skills in the other field of the plantation with the farmers.

While the adults talked, each young man toted his gun with pride, imitating his father and boasting of his shooting accomplishments.

"David," said 10-year-old Russell. "Your Grandpa bought your rifle cheap from the blacksmith. I know cause I saw the deal."

"No, no," said David, 6 years old. "Let's play soldiers. I'll be the best at shooting. No one can outshoot me. I'll be General Lee."

The eight boys formed a line, encouraged by the men around them and were sent to march around the grounds to the cheers of the hunters. They passed James standing with some townspeople, who applauded the boys as they passed. A merchant said to James, who was dressed in black pants topped with a checkered vest of black and red. A black coat hung across his shoulders. "Mighty fancy. You got more clothes than anyone wore in my day. I must be outa' style."

"In that swell outfit, some animal's gonna git you first," said another man as James moved away from them when he saw Jim and Frank. He did not wish to talk to them but eyed George, who was standing alone, looking lost and out of place.

"I'll be," James said under his breath. "He's got nerve coming here." He strolled over to the white-haired man, who was looking at everyone who passed. George saw James, and his body stiffened, as though he was in for a fight. With people around, James acted like an old friend with no recall of his October visit.

"George, what you gonna kill today? Provided you can aim."

"Ah kin aim right good."

Judah, who was talking with another group, hurried over and said, "You gotta be the leader, George. The other hunters promised to name the fox after you."

"Now, friend," said James brushing the dust from his clothes. "You were a school teacher in Charleston long 'fore you came here. You'd be the smartest master this hunt ever had."

George, annoyed at being the brunt of a joke, shook his head. He did not feel the least bit humored, especially at the word "friend" spoken by James. He felt he could not adequately deal with such a sophisticated man as James King. He had come to get away from bothersome things and hunt.

"Bein' a leader, George, you'll get the first shot," said Judah. "If you do this, I'll come back an' I'll let you shoot mah new firearm."

"Ah gots a good enough rifle," said George, looking at Judah. "Don't you worry, James. You must be careful in that vest o' yours."

Judah chimed in again. "George, you gotta be a leader. The other hunters promised to name the fox after you."

"Now, George," said James brushing the dust from his vest. "You'd be a hero. Don't you want to be a hero?"

George did not answer. His face turned red. He stood ready

to box someone should anyone make a move. He held his rifle tightly. He kept his eyes on the men who talked to James and Judah.

George was afraid. He didn't know what James and Judah would do. He did not trust them. Some of the men watched him for awhile. They seemed to know he was nervous and confused. The men close by smiled and some chuckled, even laughed. They knew King and Arnold liked to tease. They patted George on the back and walked away saying, "Come on, George. You know King and Arnold joke a lot."

The farmer did not take the matter lightly. Embarrassed by the whole situation, George slung his rifle on his back and headed down the path. "I'm goin' home," he announced loudly and walked away.

"I better go after him. Don't want any gossip to spread on how George was treated," said James.

"You better, James. He'll listen to you if you sweet-talk him, and I'll head for the woods where I can keep an eye on him."

Several of the hunters stopped to watch James pursue George. The farmer mumbled to himself under his breath as he marched steadily away from the hunters. "Ah wish they'd forget ah ever taught school. Ah liked it, but teachins' been gone from my mind many years." He thought of his near-fatal illness, which made him quit teaching. He remembered standing in the classroom by his desk, feeling faint. The room went forward and backward in his mind. He couldn't stand it, and yelled out loud. The children screamed. *That's all I remember,* he thought. *Drusilla and my parents took care of me. Mama and Daddy died soon after I got better. Ah know I felt bad, felt bad.* The doctor said all that happened brought on a bad case of depression. So

Drusilla took him away from the Charleston area to the quiet place of Indigo Springs.

King grabbed George gently by the arm trying not to hurt him as he made efforts to apologize for behaving like a school-boy. "Now, George, we've had our differences, but let's be friends, and as a friend, I apologize for any errors I made." James knew his display of acting went over well. He got the attention of the men, and they did not interfere in his making fun of George. The men stood around watching James, smiling.

George's temper got the best of him, and he swung around briskly, with the butt of his gun hitting King in the chin. The crowd let out a moan. Even George was surprised at what happened. King's feelings turned to anger as he cried out in pain and covered his chin. His jaw was not broken, but King capitalized on the situation and made it worse.

"Ohhh, ohhh," he groaned.

"James," said Judah running forward to him. "Let me help you. You're hurt."

George backed away slowly. "Hope you're not hurt too bad, but ah ain't your friend."

George stood motionless, waiting to see what King would do. He watched King moan in pain and began to feel good about himself and triumphant for the moment, ready to protect his honor if he must. A smile appeared from his lips.

"I think I need a doctor," said James in a low, moaning voice.

He took a handkerchief and patted the scratch. The hunters waited anxiously for the next move, but someone else gave the call to hunt. George seized the moment and left with the other men and looked back to see the fierce, angry eyes of the captain glaring at him. George hurried along with the other farmers.

"That the best I seen you do," said one of them.

"You held your own. Good enough against them two big ones," said another.

George hurried along with the farmers, looking back for James or Judah to follow. He was confident he had lost them. With comrades he knew, all tillers of the soil, George cherished the moment of being in their company. Sometimes in the past, many of them would be invited to Mrs. Turner's for a cool drink and pastries in her garden. They always stood apart from the others at these gatherings because of their clothes and their talk of farming. They were left out of the war discussions.

George and Drusilla always made sure they had enough when time and seasons imposed hardship. The Franklins would drive their carriage east to the Savannah River crossing, board the boat to Columbia, purchase their supplies and not be at anyone's mercy. They always had the money hidden.

The hunters by this time approached their destination on the south end of the farm. The men knew they couldn't keep up with the ones who had horses, and the men George accompanied were more interested in hunting wild turkey and small animals. The noise from the horn and the horses kept the game hidden unless the dogs sniffed it out.

Jim and Frank rode away from the rest of the riders and found a shady clearing with just enough warm sun penetrating through the trees to give off warmth on the cool ground. Jim brought along some food Lauren had packed and both men enjoyed the repast.

"Frank, in these many years since the war you've done well and have much to be thankful for," said Jim.

"I do. I owe it all to my mother who kept certain things hidden from the Yankee intruders. I think of her often now that she's gone to the Almighty. She was a great Southern lady, but just between you an' me, she told me once she didn't place complete faith in the Confederacy."

"Why was that?"

"She said so many people did not have the resources to win, or the money. The workers were too poor. Do you suppose that was true?"

Jim did not want to continue to discuss the past political feelings as he remembered the September meeting at Sam's. Instead he changed the subject.

"Say, Frank, what have you heard from Sam? I've not spoken a word to him since the meeting two months ago."

Frank thought a minute. "I'd say since the ruckus at Cokesbury, Sam lays low. You know, he and Tom were always into something. They made their money off other gamblers but bet on other things till it was gone. I suspect they owe people money and would want to get away till affairs cool down some. Tom was his confidant, and I'll bet he's a lonely man."

"Who's a lonely man?"

"Sam. Oh, Jim, haven't you heard that Tom died? I was surprised as anybody."

"Truthfully, I didn't know! I haven't seen Sam either, but my wife heard Tom was ill, which we all knew. Anyone seen Sam? Did he ever finish that conversation you and he had about some North Carolina property?"

"No, he didn't. Wondered about it myself. He probably lost it by now."

"Any gun shots or anything on Tom's body that you heard of?"

"No, nothing. That's strange. No funeral, either."

"You're right," concluded Jim. "It is a bit strange. Looks to me like Sam could head down the wrong road. A shame. He's smart and talented. Say, when are you and Betty coming to see Lauren and me?"

Jim knew he changed the subject, but he felt certain he had heard enough. He wasn't sure he could help Sam.

"Jim, it's so hard for me to travel these days. The children and the farm keep me busy. You're aware my one hand keeps me from farming. Used to have a good foreman. He wasn't mean, got their respect, and everyone worked productively. Today, I've got to drive my help. Come to think of it, I don't like goin' to town much these days. All those bad things have happened...the blacks rioting, citizens getting hurt and all the militia. People turn unchristian to each other."

"Frank, mankind has been that way since the beginning of time. Let's pray it doesn't get worse again. But what keeps me busy is working all night on cases. That does me in! The cases are piling up while I wait for Judge Mackey."

"I hear he's quite a man. I am not too sure of his character, coming from the big city of Charleston and all, but I guess he's all right."

"To be honest, I'd prefer a man who keeps better notes in court."

"Jim, Betty would never forgive me if I didn't ask about Lauren. Tell me how she is feeling."

The attorney sighed and said, "The good news is the doctor decided not to call for a long time. He plainly told both of us there was no more he could do, and Lauren will have to try to walk on her own. Believe it or not, I know she tries. I've heard her upstairs when she thinks I'm not at home. The bad news is she does not try for longer periods of time. I'm afraid after our child was stillborn she became depressed."

"I'll send Betty to see her, and they can go on an outing."

They both heard the horn sound once more, and one of the men rode up to them, urging Jim and Frank to join the party.

"Let's go. I've got to shoot something or hear from Lauren," said Jim.

"Let's catch that fox!" said Frank. Both men leaped on their horses and headed in the direction of the sound, with Jim's horse galloping in the lead.

Not far away, George stayed with the friends he knew. Jay Watkins shouted to the group. "Let's split up. Maybe we'll find game."

All the others spread out in every direction away from the big hunt. George wished he could have taken Jeff with him. Jeff was a better shot. Besides, Jeff had the patience to hunt. George walked some distance, and before he knew it, George was standing alone near a small pond in an area of the host's farm he had never seen before. He thought an animal would be along, and he'd be able to shoot it. The pine trees and the oaks vied for the sun and were as thick as cows in a pasture. George crouched behind a tree and settled himself when he was startled by a familiar voice coming directly behind him, he jumped up.

"Hey, George, I see ya. Ya got no cause to park yerself here."

George quickly turned and pointed his rifle in the direction of the sound. He waited and grumbled, "Why can't a body find some peace?"

He thought there are folks around who liked to disturb another's serenity. George blinked his eyes, but that did not help him focus any better. The woods, very thick and deeply shaded, also made it impossible for George to see for a distance. He listened intently, but no sound was heard. George knew he was a target, if a person decided to shoot. He squatted down in some bushes and shouted.

"Whacha want?"

The answer came from nearby, "Ah want you out of here."

George was scared. He recognized Judah's voice. He waited, but still did not see the black-bearded man or hear another sound. George had the greatest desire to run away, and he thought that was the message Judah wanted to convey.

"Ah hate this game. Ah refuse to play," he said softly.

He stayed low on the ground and decided to crawl quietly to another tree. He waited. He could not hear anything. Nothing moved. He was hungry and could no longer put off eating. Soon it was getting dark. Still there was no voice and no other sounds. The moon was round and full and illuminated the sky.

"Ah don' like sneakin' around firin' shots in the air." He waited and remembered he had some bread and meat Drusilla fixed for him to eat. He took it out of a sack as cautiously as possible, devoured the food. He gulped it down; then slowly stood up. "If nothin' fires at my hat, I'm goin' to sneak aroun' the lake. Gotta get outta here. It's dark but that ol moon is shinin'. Guess maybe I'll be safe."

He crouched down and crawled in the tall grass to get near the bushy area surrounding the lake. He felt safer when he saw a farmer who was also heading home.

CHAPTER 7

No night seemed prettier than Christmas Eve. George, confident of this thoughtful pronouncement, stood at the small, square cabin window. He looked longingly out toward the sandbank where bits of moonbeams twinkled through the tree branches, causing the granules to sparkle. He surveyed the stars, believing they had never shone brighter, the moon glossier, and the darkness like a mistress, never more inviting. The bachelor reflected in an air of anticipation he felt, lingering in the shadows, that peace and joy would mingle with excitement, keeping the momentum of goodness alive and well.

He continued to gaze at the darkness as he pressed his face against the glass. He cupped his dry-skinned hands over his eyes hoping to see some distant figure. He did not know who; maybe someone to visit him and Drusilla on Christmas Eve. If the moon stayed shiny, George knew he'd eventually glimpse a raccoon or an opossum or two scurrying about their business.

"Look, Drusilla, there goes one now, a raccoon. Ah can tell he's a'headin' for his tree."

George turned and waited for Drusilla to answer, but she busied herself in the little space she had on the small table, making sausage patties and watching the biscuits in the oven. She was too occupied to bother with George, whose nature tended toward sentimentality and melancholia this time of the year. He in turn knew his sister was good to him even though he questioned her personal social graces.

The year had gone fast, he thought. An experienced farmer, George believed he profited from his crops with this year's swift passing. It pleased him more than his sister, who never commented about money but always took the cash, concealing it in the fur-covered chest so well hidden in her tiny room under her fluffy mattress.

George remembered three days ago when he gave Jeff an unexpected bonus. He slipped over the sandbank while Drusilla was cooking. "Jeff, Jeff," he said in a moderate tone. The older man, who was about ready to go into his cabin, turned around.

"Ah got a little something for you. Take it quick an' don't tell, ever!" He slid some extra coins into Jeff's hand.

George believed in rewarding a kind and good servant and knew Jeff's son was growing up and could use some things he had hoped for as a boy.

The farmer turned again and watched Drusilla fry the sausage. He noticed the glow of the firelight, which softened his sister's facial features. Drusilla, as a young girl, seemed attractive to young men. She stood tall and slender, with a creamy complexion that did not show wrinkles unless one was close to her. She even had a sense of humor. Her brother sensed her loneliness since she lost her sweetheart years ago. Maybe the ordeal and grief caused her personality to change. He wondered.

Just then George spied the neatly tied brown package waiting for him on the cupboard shelf. He forgot about it with his Christmas dreaming. Like a child in want on Christmas morning, George grabbed it, carefully unwrapping the paper so as not to tear it in case he wanted to wrap the knife again. He looked at the contents in delight, for it was the gift he bought for himself at Turner's store and paid off by secretly holding a few extra coins aside each time Jeff went to market.

"What silly thing have you got there?" said Drusilla, stretching her body as far as she could to detect the contents.

George laid the contents in his palm, admiring it before showing Drusilla.

"This knife be jus' the right size for me," he said softly.

He turned and looked at Drusilla. "It's got lots a' uses," he said.

"What ya gonna use that for? It's so little. Can't cut rope to tie the horse."

George studied every detail of the weapon before slipping it into his right pocket. He didn't answer.

Drusilla busied herself by gathering the supper utensils and wiping up the grease spots from the stove. The light from the tallow candle puffed out, and she replaced it, using the candle on top of her stove, leaving a film of darkness in that corner. When the meal was served, she snuffed out the other candles except for the one on the table. "Everything's done," said Drusilla snifting out the other candles.

George's imagination led him to wonder what Gideon and his family were doing for Christmas. Drusilla nudged him to fold his hands. "Ah guess I better pray out loud," he said. "We give thanks, oh Lord, for what we are about to receive for our bodies. Make us pure like the Babe born in Bethlehem, we pray. Amen."

They picked at their food. Neither spoke. The coffee was hot, and George sipped it carefully. He glanced again at the small window, realizing how beautifully the candlelight flickered in the glass. It hypnotized him. For a few seconds Drusilla stopped eating. She listened, but George remained deep in thought. Drusilla listened again to the strange inexplicable sound very close to the house. She could not place the sound.

Drusilla took a few bites of her biscuit, but before she could swallow her food, a knock on the door startled them both. They stared at each other in total astonishment. George pushed back his chair and almost fell. His sister held his arm, as if telling him not to answer. The knock came again. George looked at Drusilla. Both of them felt uneasy.

"Who'd you ask?" he whispered. Drusilla shook her head no. "Ah wonder who is stand'n outside," he stated.

Then a cheerful voice called, "It's Christmas."

George's sister held her hand out to hold her brother back, but George said, "Gideon. Gideon, is it you?" He pulled away to unlatch the door.

For a few seconds the older Franklin strained his eyes trying to make out the silent adult-size figure somewhere in front of him on the hewn-stone slab. Darkness covered whoever was standing there. "Gideon, I can't see you clear. Come in."

"Yeeeee!" screamed Drusilla, who saw a weapon come up, ready to hit her brother. Before George recognized the intruder, an arm swung around with a club and planted a sharp blow to his skull. A stream of blood began to flow over his snow-white hair and ruddy complexion. He dropped to the floor, unconscious and defenseless, like a soldier stabbed in battle.

Drusilla gasped and almost choked on the mouthful of biscuit crumbs in her throat. She coughed up the little pieces and arose from her chair in disbelief. Her brother had fallen down on the stone, as if stricken with a paralysis.

Drusilla moaned, sweeping her arms toward the doorway, ready to attack the villain. She had the urge to protect herself from an evil force she could not perceive. She stepped toward the door. It occurred to her to escape to her tiny room and latch the door and push the bed against it. She attempted to scream. All she could do was cough up some more food particles. This stopped her from yelling for Jeff.

Although it was a certainty that a person of her size and thin frame could manage at all, she had the determination to succeed. Within seconds, the attacker stepped in, swinging his club toward her head. Her arms swept upward with her hands trying to shield herself and duck lower with her body. Without a doubt, an unrecognizable, mysterious man had full control, and struck Drusilla with force. She fell to her knees and then to the floor. Immediately, she knew the tallow candle was out.

"Boss," called the man with the club. The other man stepped over George's body, feeling his pockets, and then partially closed the door against it, pushing George's corpse close to the edge of the stone.

"Light this other candle from the fireplace," said the second intruder. Then he motioned to his accomplice to begin the search for money as he picked George's pockets. The attacker broke every dish in the cupboard, not caring where the pieces smashed to the floor.

Both men laughed. Their spirits soared as they tore the crudely nailed cabinet boards apart with their bare hands.

"Boss, Boss, the false bottoms got money," said the attacker.

"What did I tell you? Get your pockets full, and I will too," said the second intruder.

Some money fell to the floor.

"Let's split the furniture open. Don't leave any objects. Break them open. There could be money inside," said the second intruder excitedly. "Hurry, we've got to keep moving. Looks like they both are out."

They tore open or broke whatever happened to be in their way, not caring where the pieces fell. The splinters landed in Drusilla's hair. Her plain, gray clothes were splotched with blood and wood and splinters of glassware. Nails from the broken boards covered her legs and tore her cotton stockings to pieces.

The intruders, swift and cunning, were soon in Drusilla's small room. The second intruder said, "Light another candle while I start to rip everything I can get my hand on, but remember the chest is mine."

They found money everywhere, to the delight of both men. It was in the dresser, hidden in the loose floor boards, in picture frames, and every place imaginable in Drusilla's small room.

"She didn't have many clothes but look how many bills I found in the hem of her skirts!" said the second intruder, smiling. He could hardly stuff more into his pockets.

By this time the robbers were utterly ecstatic and making gleeful noises. In their joy and excessive greed, they did not hear Drusilla whine in the other room.

Her eyes opened. She immediately had the sensation of having been pricked all over, especially on her feet. Drusilla started to become conscious after a few seconds and tears rolled down her cheeks. The awful picture of George flashed before her eyes. She turned her head toward the door. Her neck ached. In the darkness she could tell someone had fallen on the hewn stone. The glow from the moon outlined George's still body. The thought flashed through her mind, why is he not moving, helping me?

She ached with pain as the attack on George played in her mind. Someone struck him. He fell. She lay still for a moment, afraid to move. She felt tortured as she whimpered, "Can I move? Is anyone here? Is the robber still here?"

"*Help! Help!*" she tried to call but to no avail. Her throat, still sore and scratchy, felt hot and burning.

Drusilla listened intently. Her vision stayed cloudy and dim. She tried to focus in the dark room. In the next few moments she realized the darkness covered her like a warm blanket, and for a second, the safety of it comforted her. Her body shook. She asked herself, *What will I do if the stranger remains in the room close by?*

Drusilla waited. She listened and stayed motionless. She touched the wet blood on her face. She felt a few drops on her neck. She found she could raise her head slightly. A tinge of pain crossed her brow, causing her to roll over with her hands covering her face in agony. More pain came rapidly, like bullets from a gun. Her head went down and her body started to shake again.

Someone was nearby. She waited; then she heard loud shuffling sounds. There were footsteps. One person had boots and another had no shoes and large feet that shifted on her wooden floor. Consciously, she knew the noise came from her room. It sounded as though more than one person had entered her chamber. Drusilla wanted to cry out, but her head ached and once more she felt excruciating pain.

In time, her eyes focused in the darkness, and Drusilla saw the faint glow of the fireplace and the candlelight shining from her room. She immediately felt invaded! How dare someone, anyone trespass her private quarters! Even her brother slept on mats near the door. Her belongings! They were no one else's. Why are they here? What do these people want? How many are here? The figures seemed difficult to detect, shuffling about, making noises. Maybe they are tearing my bedclothes!

Again, Drusilla tried to scream, but her throat was tight and the pain flashed through her body, soaring all over. The discomfort, too much to bear at this moment, made her think of death.

"No, no, I never thought it would be this way. George! You cannot help me. George! Oh, Lord! George!" she spoke, weeping.

When the pain ceased after a few minutes, Drusilla heard voices.

"Massa, here. What's dis?" said a man in a deep voice.

"I hope it's more money," said the other man.

One voice was familiar to Drusilla. She recognized it. This gave her strength to rise, and in trying, she wondered if she'd be able to endure.

She heard one man say, "Get the things you got in your pocket. I ain't got two hands. I'll hold this end and you work it."

"Yes suh."

Drusilla wondered what they were referring to. She put her hands under her chest, attempting to push herself up but cut her hands on a piece of broken glass. She grabbed the overturned table leg and pulled her body half-way up, but the pain returned. She sank to the floor. She waited breathless for the pain to subside.

Again, she heard the familiar voice mutter something inaudible about the "fur-covered chest." Drusilla wanted to cry to George for help, but it was no use. She knew he was dead.

"Help. Help." Drusilla strained her voice, but the sound weakened. "Jeff, Jeff, come. I need you."

She wondered if she could walk out the door and over the sandbar. Then she heard the men shout with glee.

"Here it is!" They laughed excitedly, like children.

Drusilla's heart pounded. She stood on her feet. She grasped the short message that they had found her carefully-concealed chest buried so well under her bed and tied with ropes. Blood dripped down her face. She wiped her eyes and staggered toward the bedroom to save her only priceless possession.

The two greedy participants in crime continued to scramble furiously for more money. Unsatisfied with the cash they discovered hidden in the other room, the murderers reached out with their knives to cut loose the ropes that held the chest.

One murderer said, "I know it's here. Hurry."

"You smilin', boss."

"Sure, I'm smiling! Why not? This is what I've been looking for. Hurrah! This wasn't too bad a work for you and me. We got what we came for and more! Break this lock!" One blow by the bigger man and the lock was broken.

"Lordy, Ah never seen so much money at one time!"

The men grinned and sifted their hands through the coins and bills, stuffing their big pockets.

"This is great! I'll be able to manage nicely for awhile now and won't have to bother anyone. Whoa, whoa. Saints, look what's coming!"

Just then the shape of Drusilla's bloody hands made a silhouette in the candlelight against the wall. They were set in motion to grab the one man she knew. He gasped at the sight of her stepping into the room.

When the black man saw her, he was stunned for a few seconds, exclaiming, "Ah thought I killed her, boss!"

The man's partner kept the club next to him and cuddled it like a toy.

"Gimmee that club," said the man with one arm. The man fumbled for it and the club fell to the floor.

"Curses. Get it for me quickly."

His partner grabbed for it and handed the thick stick to him and stepped aside.

Drusilla tried to talk. She wanted to shout his name to the roof tops. She lunged to get a hold of him and choke him for what he was doing. The former soldier had no tender feelings for Drusilla, or any sympathy for her. In an instant, Drusilla's bloody, bony hands reached out to grab the person she knew. He swung the club at her forehead. She slumped across the bed. The blood rushed out of her skull and her legs dangled motionless across the bed. The partner, sweating and full of fear and trepidation, at the thin and bloody figure lying on the bed, and stood motionless against the wall.

"Aren't you relieved the old woman's dead?" said Sam.

"Yes, suh."

The partner stood back and let Sam grab the rest of the money. "Come on. You can take a little bit right away. We're in a hurry to go."

The black man obliged while Sam stood for a moment, watching Drusilla's legs dangle motionlessly.

"Next time, if there is one, hit your victim harder," said the boss angrily, throwing the club at his partner. "Let's get outta here. I need a drink. I want no part of her again. I'll take the rest of the dollars and coins for my trouble."

He grabbed all the money he could muster with his only hand and started for the door. He believed his right arm was good for something. He jumped over George's body and quickly turned, trying to follow the same path as before.

"Hay, wahr ya goin' so fass?" called his companion as he proceeded to run after his comrade in crime into the darkness that devoured them In their hurry, they knocked over a pig pen on one side of the yard. The men cussed.

In the darkness, Sam tripped. He accidentally dropped a knife and, not seeing or feeling it in the dark, hurried ahead.

"Speed up," he said to his partner, far behind. "Let's cut across the field to the horses."

The murderers ran faster, and the former slave tossed the bloody club into some bushes.

CHAPTER 8

Frank awakened and through a crack in the shutter saw the dawn creep quietly as it always does on Christmas morning. In a whisper, moving his lips, he prayed for a minute.

"Lord, I am thankful for this bounty and the farm I love. For this gift, I promise to treat my help better and do something special for them on this jubilant morning. In Your name, I pray."

He listened carefully to a faint noise coming from outside the room. He heard the patter of small feet coming toward the bedroom, then the voices of the household guests too excited to sleep any longer. Frank gently nudged Betty, who awoke slowly and mumbled, "Is it morning already? Goodness, it came fast."

She stretched her body against his and hugged and kissed her husband. He responded, but the peace and quiet endured only a short while. It was overshadowed by the children bursting into the room, filling it with vim and vigor and jumping up and down on the bed.

"I can jump higher than Lucy. Lucy, look at me," said Frank III.

"You're cheating. Mama, he's cheating. Look at him," said his sister, Lucy.

"Children, it's Christmas. What will our guests say with all the noise?" said Frank.

"Let's dress and get downstairs to the parlor as fast as we

can for surprises," said Betty, who received no argument from anyone.

They left the room and Frank began his morning ritual.

After the feast of Christmas food and presents, the guests seated themselves in the parlor while Betty handed out the hymnals. Their hosts gave a blessing, and while everyone remained silent, Frank read the Christmas story from Luke. Adam, Betty's cousin, said, "It's my favorite time. Let's sing carols. I'll start the music."

"I'm going to smoke my pipe," said Frank. "Anyone for the porch with me at this early morning hour?"

"I'll come with you," said an older relative, Uncle Matt, from rural Georgia. "Can't sing anyway."

They opened the front door and stepped onto the porch. The happy sounds of children and the laughter pleased Frank and Uncle Matt as they lit their pipes, but the noise was constant and Frank closed the door, standing in silence looking out at his farm with pleasure. In a short time, Uncle Matt pointed to the haze lifting while the sun worked slowly and steadily to dry the wet ground.

"You know, Uncle Matt, mist is a form of purity, a blessed refreshment for crops and man."

"Uh, huh," said Uncle Matt, too interested in his pipe.

"See that far field out there, the one that has the white fence around it? Well, it's my favorite spot, and I plan to put the wheat there. Don't you think it's a good idea?"

"Yup! You got lots of good ideas," said Uncle Matt, still enjoying his pipe.

"Yes," Frank proclaimed, taking a deep breath and grinning pleasantly. "It's going to be a blessed Christmas."

Then he leaned against the railing, raising his arm and pointing out the fields and the long distance of his acreage to his relative. "You know, when my mother was alive, she dreamed of having a bigger farm like this. We had the land. She was in the process of doing this, expanding the farm. We had all the help then, but the war came and it was impossible. Most of our good slaves left just as quick as they could. But it's been several years now, and the help that stayed sure worked hard. So, today being Christmas, I planned some extra food for them."

Uncle Matt sat forward in the chair and began talking about his Georgia farm. During the course of their conversation, Betty came out and brought hot coffee for the men. She stood close to Frank and admired the scenery with him.

"The winter's left the area bleak," said Betty, "but the land shows the promise of spring. I hope you'll come back in the spring, Uncle Matt."

As the illustrious veteran surveyed his grounds, he again pointed toward the path to demonstrate what crops would be planted. "You know, spring will be a good time. We'll put the vegetables over there and get some more fruit trees there."

When he turned in the direction of the neighboring fields, he spied someone in the distance hobbling hurriedly down the road. The veteran studied the outline of the man as he came closer and closer—stumbling, half walking, then running, holding his side. Frank, Betty and Uncle Matt walked down the steps to meet this lone caller whose words could not be heard from a distance.

"Betty, can you make out who it is?"

"Not just yet. I can't see a long distance. Uncle Matt, can you tell who it is?"

"You're asking the wrong one. Haven't got the eyesight I used to have."

"Seems to be in a hurry, whoever it is…why, it must be Jeff! For a long time, I haven't seen him come this way. I wonder what's the matter?" said Frank, who could barely hear Jeff speak.

"Capt'n, Capt'n. Come quick, come quick. Marse George… all bloody, all bloody."

Jeff gasped for breath and almost collapsed into the Fuller's one arm. He was perspiring in spite of the cooler weather. Jeff appeared to be in a state of shock.

"Why, I do suspect something terrified him!" said Uncle Matt, who grabbed Jeff's other arm to steady him. "Look at his eyes."

Jeff gazed at the people on the porch who saw the excitement from the window and came out to watch with interest. Jeff could barely talk. Frank steadied the old man while a child brought a cup of water.

Jeff nodded his head in thanks and drank it. He tried again desperately to speak, but the words would not come. He breathed irregularly.

"Jeff, you've got to lean against this tree and get your breath. It'll be all right soon. You'll catch your breath."

"Here's a dry cloth to wipe your face, Jeff," said Betty, handing him a towel.

"Now you're getting calmer. What happened, Jeff? We want to know," said Frank.

In a short time, with some coaxing from Betty and Uncle Matt, the former slave began to relate what he wanted to say. "Poor Marse George be down in da cabin doorway…and Miz

Drusilla is not answerin' mah call." The old man bowed his head and wiped his eyes. Then he folded his hands in despair.

"Frank, something's wrong," said Betty. "It sounds scary!"

"Mah son done went ta make da fire an' carry water ta da cabin. Early mornin' was real foggy at dat time." Jeff stopped talking. He could feel his heart pound.

Frank urged him to go on, and led him to a chair someone brought from the porch.

Jeff looked up at the captain. "Mah son come up ta da house and saw Marse George a lyin' on the doorstep all bloody. He ran to mah house. He so scared."

Frank, both astonished and puzzled by such a happening, knew quite well that Jeff was never known as a liar.

"Are you sure you told us everything, Jeff? Is there more? What did you say of Miss Drusilla?"

"Capt'n, capt'n, Ah did'n go...did'n go into da house. We's tellin' all da white folks first. Dats what I saw. Dats what I saw. Ah's scared, scared."

* * * * *

Frank stood near the huge stone where George lay in a circle of blood alone. The dead man's body was pushed against the cabin door. He gazed at George's still remains and wondered why anyone would want to give such an unmerciful blow to the head.

"You poor man. You did no one any harm, but you were a peculiar fella sometimes," Frank said out loud. "I admit I don't know how to take you, dead or alive. We haven't spoken for many years, but it's a shame you had to come to this."

Nobody in town except maybe the farmers understood the

murdered man, but they certainly bore him no malice. Most folks believed that he and his sister were miserly, and at times uncompassionate toward other people's problems. *But to murder him...the act was uncalled for,* thought Frank.

Frank stood right in front of the Franklin cabin. He realized that this was the first time he had ever stood set foot on the Franklin property. The quarrel his mother had with George and the blue dye he grew for her from seed, came into his mind as though it were yesterday. *It's no use to bring old wounds to mind,* he thought.

He cleared his mind of any bad thoughts and looked at the Franklin home carefully. The place was old and small, and in need of a great deal of repair. He looked over at George's body apprehensively and stared through the door which was ajar. He saw the huge fireplace and knew it was more than big enough for a small room, but with all the cracks in the wood, Frank knew the home must have been cold in the winter. There must have been drafts all around.

No additions were made to the place—no fancy curtains or pictures, and if there happened to be any mementos, they must have been discarded and broken on the floor with all the glass and debris.

Frank, hearing a rustling sound, turned around. "What the...? Who's there?"

"Hay Frank, it's me. Bob Nickels. I got back a few days ago! Remember me?" He came around the sandbank with his hands in his pockets and the same smile on his round face. He wore a cap, which covered his blond hair. His coat was wrinkled and too long for him. He trudged toward Frank. When he came close, the men smiled and hugged each other.

"Bob, I thought we lost you in Tennessee."

"Like I said, I got home here a few days ago. My mother was sick for a long time. Jeff's son let me know what happened here. Since I live so close, I came right over. I've been here for a little while. No one else was here yet, and I looked about the place. Isn't it awful? I couldn't enter the cabin, but I guess we better go in. I'm afraid what we'll find if we do. There are a few things around the grounds you better see too."

"I can't believe this either. Nothing like this ever happened here. It's scary and brutal. Has Dr. Waddell been notified?"

"Yes," said Bob. "Hope it doesn't take too long to find him."

Frank began to feel an uneasiness deep within because of the distressful task ahead. "Well, Bob, which one of us is going to be the first to enter?"

"What difference does it make? You lead and I'll follow."

They cautiously entered the cabin slowly stepping inside, afraid of what they might find. Frank felt queasy in battle, but this was a different battle at home on Christmas Day. Frank realized he never felt a sense of personal warmth toward the Franklins ever since the bitter argument years ago.

"You know, Bob, I confess I never felt a friendship toward the Franklins, but I do feel some pity toward Drusilla, who really got little out of life because of her own stinginess."

"Oh, I'd see her on occasion here or there. Just humored her a bit. Sometimes she'd smile."

A horrible thought entered Frank's mind. Maybe they deserved their fate; but on second thought, he said, "No one deserves to be killed unless it's in war."

"Yeah, from the looks of things right here there musta been a battle going on."

Both men turned around when they heard the brakes of a wagon and a family of four stepped down. They gasped at the body of George on the hewn stone. Soon other neighbors came, some running, some walking, a few on horseback and more buggies parked everywhere. Many were curious and remained strangely quiet. They whispered among themselves.

Some gasps were heard as they saw the body in the partially open door, but the crowd respected Frank and Bob standing inside the entrance and did not venture too close. A few women wiped their eyes. Several children of various ages stood gawking at the body. They made sounds of "oh" and "ah." They found their friends and stood in several groups, watching and waiting to see if the body would rise up and walk.

The impact of the murder did not fully materialize in the minds of the onlookers.

One farmer who took his hat off, viewing the body said, "Why, I knew George when he first came here as a young man. He was a nice fella an' worked hard. Don't know why anyone would do this."

Another replied, "I met George through his nephew, Gideon. Say, did anyone notify him? I better go an' get him."

One of the ladies said, "George was sentimental about things. Drusilla was always in church every Sunday. That's as Christian as a body can get. Don't know what happened, but it's a terrible scene!"

Some young girl spoke. "Just like the war. Killin' and more killin.' When's everyone gonna stop?"

A group of new arrivals talked to the ones who had already arrived on the murder scene. They talked of the past and the Franklins. Many knew them as upstanding Christians at church and not gossiping about anyone. The people continued to watch and whisper and wait for the sheriff or officials.

Frank thought of his own past. He knew how promising and bright the future appeared to him attending Edinburgh University in Scotland, but the war in 1861, the battles, and the loss of his arm changed his whole way of thinking. He wanted no more suffering. He was sure of that.

A big-bearded man spoke up. "Can we come in too and see what happened?"

"What shall we do? If we let them in before we see it, the place will look much worse than it is now," said Frank to Bob.

"I know. You're right! Let me talk to the crowd and tell them we have some official business with the family till they get here," said Bob. He walked out and found the group willing to co-operate.

At that moment, Frank glanced at Jeff near the sandbank. His shoulders were bent over, his head bowed and his hands dangling lifeless at this side. Frank's felt sympathetic toward the older man. What would Jeff and his family do? Perhaps the former slave felt the saddest of anyone, he thought.

A couple of men from town approached Jeff. They wanted to ask him some questions. He heard them but did not answer.

"Jeff, did ja do somethin' bad?" said one.

"Did ja see anybody?" said the other. "When did you discover the body?"

Frank called out, "Jeff, let all the neighbors know you did a good deed."

In a short period of time the men dispersed through the crowd. More and more curiosity seekers came. Some wagons drove to the scene with several farmers and their families and people never seen before in the community. The crowd became restless for news and talked loudly. One woman said to another friend, tying her bonnet, "It looks like murder to me from the way he's a lying there. What do you think? Somebody must know something."

"I'm not sure. This place has an odor. There's blood around. Don't you smell it? Maybe we should get outta here!"

"Maybe you're right. Let's go way over there. Those people have been talking since we came, and it looks like they know what they're talkin' about."

The children began to run around the grounds. Some teased the horses. By noon a crowd stood directly outside the Franklin cabin, conversing and waiting for news of how the Franklins died. Restless teenagers tired of waiting ran everywhere and played hide 'n seek with the younger children. A few onlookers, too frightened to move, gaped at everything and everyone. Jeff stood back from the crowd. Frank, Bob, and a small party of known community leaders, chosen by Bob, entered the rustic dwelling.

George's body, stepped over like broken glass by the chosen few entering the Franklin quarters, was the object of stares and conversation. By this time the people had come close enough to notice the blood had dried on his skull and the torn clothing still covering his body.

The small group in the cabin edged their way forward as if entering some inner sanctum and crept about cautiously because of all the broken glass and debris covering the floor, with boards and nails strewn everywhere. Chairs were turned over. George's bed roll was covered with debris.

Bob tapped Frank and pointed to Drusilla's body lying face down across the bed in her tiny room with her feet touching the floor. The men stared in silence.

"Hey! Everyone!" said a man outside. "Doc Waddell's coming. Make way for him."

Immediately the doctor knelt down and examined George's skull. Next he checked Drusilla's.

"Gentlemen," the doctor announced, "the Franklins were struck in the head with a blunt instrument, which broke both their skulls."

The crowd nodded in agreement and passed the word to the rest of the people, who summarized it as a swift, hard blow. Frank pointed to the table, which contained the remains of a partially eaten meal rather dried and uneatable by this time.

"The murders must have been committed at the supper hour on Christmas Eve," said Frank.

As the word spread, people began filling the doorway and then the small room. They pushed, and others started arguments, but as many people as possible were determined to get in the Franklin's cabin, which many only saw from the outside.

One older lady with a pink cap said, "Just look at the mess. I thought Drusilla was neater than this."

"Marybelle," said her husband, "I'll just bet the murderers did this. I wonder what they were looking for?"

"Dear," said the man's wife, "the Franklins had money. Look, there's some on the floor. Let's get some." The crowd scrambled to pick up the scattered coins.

"Stop!" shouted Frank. "That money is for Gideon, their nephew."

Some people dropped their findings but some did not.

"The murderer or murderers sure made a very thorough search for money," said Dr. Waddell. "Look! A few bills are scattered there under the pile of clothes."

Again, at the word of money, some neighbors lunged to retrieve the bills.

"Wait! We said the money's for Gideon and his family," said Frank as he, Bob and the doctor held them back.

"Yes, remember, what's left goes to the relatives of the Franklins. It costs to bury them," said Bob, pushing and desperately pleading to those who assembled, and shoved them back.

Frank spotted James and Judah conversing with some men. He waved hoping to get their attention and assist by keeping the crowd under control.

"James. Judah. I need your help. James. Judah." He waited a second and called again, "James. Judah."

The men paid no attention. They were too busy watching Jeff.

"It's time to go now, people. You saw what terrible events happened here. It's time to go out now," said Doc Waddell.

"Yes, we're all going outside. Let's clear the room and ask questions outdoors," said Frank.

As soon as everyone was outside, Frank searched George's pockets and found nothing. Bob and Doc Waddell set the body against the door again. A scream filled the air near the persimmon bushes. Everyone, surprised by the unexpected alarm, ran after all the children who got to the girl near the persimmons first.

"Look there," she said. "A knife." Bob hurriedly stepped into the bushes and retrieved George's knife.

"Frank," called Bob. "Come closer. Notice the uneven cut of the branches."

They studied the cuts and said nothing to each other.

At that precise moment, Gideon and his family arrived, and the crowd politely stood aside. Gideon's wife cried and the children clung to her skirts as soon as they saw George's body. Several women comforted the mourners while Gideon went in the cabin alone.

"Jeff," said Frank, "I think you should get to Greenwood to notify the magistrate who can act as coroner."

"Ah'll go with him," said Judah, stepping out of the crowd. Jeff left as fast as he could.

In their absence, James edged his way to some prominent Abbeville townspeople standing to one side of the crowd. "Good day." He took off his hat to the ladies. "I am as distressed as I think you are over this terrible happening. It's hard to believe a servant who lives close by would not hear a sound. Funny how that could happen. I didn't know that Jeff couldn't hear."

A tall gentleman from town said, "Can't say one way or the other. I find it hard to imagine anyone to be such a sound sleeper when your master may need you."

The small group agreed with each other.

Later in the afternoon, when Jeff returned with the coroner, these same citizens became suspicious of Jeff. He stood alone near the sandbar saddened and depressed. The decision made among the group was to arrest him.

Two men cautiously approached him from behind so they

wouldn't attract his attention, but the former slave noticed and realized James was standing very near, watching his every move. Jeff had never stood so close to this man before, and he marveled at something he was not aware of in the past. James resembled Sam, with the exception that James was not bald, but taller, and, of course, had both arms.

Judah casually stood next to Jeff, who soon realized trouble was brewing. He saw how Judah's black beard twitched in nervous delight. Jeff tried to get his mind off the killing and watched the crowds trample the Franklin premises. *You best be careful. Miz Drusilla will get upset,* he thought. *Maybe if I slip away to mah cabin, these men will leave me alone.* He was kept in the middle by force. James nudged his companion, and they compelled Jeff to walk into the sand pile.

"You, walk this way, boy," Judah said. "We ain't goin' to let you go!"

Before Frank could stop them, the men arrested Jeff and his family. "Yeah, yeah," shouted the crowd, who took him to the county jail in Abbeville.

* * * * *

Five weeks later, Jeff and his family stood in the courtroom of Judge Thomas J. Mackey who opened the Court of General Sessions. The Davids were tried for the murder of the Franklins. When they were arraigned and charged with the crime, the judge noted they had no counsel, so he assigned the person he believed to be a sympathetic lawyer, James Benet.

In his office, Jim talked to his clerk, Billy. "I feel inadequate about being assigned to this case. I know so little about it except what I read in the Abbeville Medium newspaper that told of the impending trial and Jeff's mistreatment in jail. I will have to see this man and his family. I can't believe that Jeff would have done such a thing as murder his employers."

"Perhaps, Jim, you could talk to some of the people who were at the scene," said Billy. I understand people came from all directions. Maybe someone saw something or heard something from someone that could be pertinent to this case. The paper stated that lots of people visited the gravesite at Bethlehem Church too."

"A good idea. On second thought, instinct tells me I better see Jeff first and find out what this is all about. I imagine the poor man is worried and afraid. I vow to do the best for them, and I hope I can do it. Billy, this case becomes a distressful situation when many people pronounce Jeff guilty."

"It seems to be going that way," said Billy when Jim went out the door.

In the cell, Jeff and Mandy looked tired, thin, and drawn. His unclean clothes had an odor to them. Otherwise Jim could find no signs of mistreatment.

"Marse Benet, we sorry for what happened. Terrible sorry. We cries together. Marse George and Miz Drusilla is gone," said Jeff, teary eyed.

"Jeff, it's very important for you to tell me everything you know about the night the Franklins were killed. Start at the beginning," said Jim.

Jeff and his wife sat on the only bunk. Jeff kept his hands folded the entire time.

"Marse Benet, we's home all da time. We eats a bit o' chicken late at night for supper cause it was Christmas Eve. We saved it from another time dat Miz Drusilla gave it to us. My wife, Jasper, my son, and ah sang softly some carols taught us by Miz Drusilla a long time ago."

"About what time did you eat?"

"We ain'ts got no clock, Marse Benet. Ah know it be dark time. Yes, dark time."

"Did you hear any noise then?"

"No, sir." Mandy shook her head no in agreement.

"Did you hear any noise during the night?"

"Marse Benet, we's so tired and thankful to da Lord that we's got a place and work dat we fall in a sound sleep. We bundles up n' keeps a fire fo' warmth. We speak of da Christ child. He's lyin' in a poor humble manger like us, Marse Benet. Den we closes our eyes."

The Davids claimed they never asked or questioned the Franklins about anything and in turn were treated fairly. Jim asked a few more routine questions and concluded to himself that the Davids were innocent. Afterwards, in the days that followed, Jim inquired everywhere but found no witness to testify in the David' behalf.

In the meantime, the Abbeville Press and Banner questioned and conversed with many people to publish their article about the Franklins. The paper stated and Jim read:

Wednesday, December 26, 1877

DOUBLE MURDER

Two Old Persons Clubbed to Death

A murder has taken place near Simms Cross Roads in this county at a little farmhouse known in the Indigo Springs area.

Both unmarried and both up in years.

No servants lived in the house.

Neighbors were Negroes who lived 200 yards away. Son of one of the Negroes discovered bodies on the way toward Franklins.

Boy saw door open and saw George Franklin, up in years. was dead on the floor, and the boy did not go into the house, but ran back to his parents a distance of 200 yards across the road and reported the facts.

Previously Negroes had been engaged in hog killing.

Negro father sent for white neighbors and Dr. H. G. Waddell.

He found George Franklin killed by a blow to the head which crushed the skull. His sister was found in an adjoining room with feet on floor and rest of body on the bed. Her head had been crushed by a blow from a stick in much the same manner as her brother.

Murder was committed at supper and coffee only partly drunk.

From blood on the floor it would appear sister was struck at table and she afterwards recovered sufficiently to get to the adjoining room where the fatal blow occurred. Wounds bled profusely—covered the floor and saturated the bed.

The instrument of death was a green persimmon club about two inches in diameter and two inches long, which had been cut near the house (in the woods) with a pocket knife. Bloody white hairs found on it and found near a stump where stick was cut. At the back of house, two distinct sets of footprints were observed fleeing to the woods.

Object was plunder and robbery. Robbers opened trunk with a poker and ransacked it, scattering papers, dishes and bureau drawers—pulled and ransacked. Murderers took the money but did not get it all because $500 in greenbacks was found in trunk's false bottom.

Hundreds of persons visit Franklin farm and grave daily. Buried at Bethlehem Church on Saturday.

CHAPTER 9

A few days before the trial, the Honorable Judge Thomas Mackey stood silently at attention near the prospective site of the Abbeville Confederate Memorial. His long, dusty, black coat, slightly big for his short stature, had been rolled up at the sleeves and made the sleeves even with the cuffs of his suit. He felt satisfied with the way he dressed but promised himself a new coat when he returned to Charleston at the end of the David trial.

He looked sternly at the site chosen for the statue and nodded his round head. He took off his hat and placed it on his heart in a moment of silence. His pudgy fingers held it tightly, as if it would blow away, but there was no wind that day.

An old gentleman out strolling with his cane spotted the judge in deep concentration and came up to him from behind. "Mighty glad you are here, your honor. How you been all these months?"

"Oh, thank you. Fine, fine," said Mackey as he quickly turned. "Wouldn't miss it for the world. You, sir? How have you been?" The judge tried to remember his name.

"All right, if it weren't for these legs...could use a new pair. What do you think of our statue site?"

"It will be a fine tribute for our men who sacrificed and died and gave for the Confederacy in the War Between the

States. It's a great opportunity for us to salute them."

The old man saw the judge thinking of his next words. He looked at him with curiosity and waited. After a few seconds he interrupted his honor's thoughts by saying, "You know, it's the money. People have to give more, or we won't get the money for the statue. Have you given, judge?"

"Uh, no, not yet. But I will, I will. I'll do it real soon, real soon."

"A good day to you, your honor," said the man, smiling as he walked away.

No name came to the judge's mind, and he walked a few steps and put on his hat. His hair became ruffled, and he smoothed it over his bald spot. He didn't mind, for he believed this made him look distinguished and educated.

Mackey liked the town. He decided it suited him to be in a quiet place at this time of the morning. He moved to the far side of the benches where the future statue would stand. He speculated it would be good place to be alone and rest after his long journey from Charleston. Inevitably, his thoughts were interrupted by a four-horse stage coach bringing in passengers.

He watched the people descending the coach. An older woman rubbed her back and took the arm of a waiting friend. Mackey momentarily chuckled to himself and remembered his rugged but uneventful journey from his home to start his circuit of court cases.

He recalled the road being dusty and dirty because of the unseasonably dry weather. On the stage, before it departed, the judge brushed his Prince Albert coat, paying no attention to the only passenger on board. Ordinarily, he accepted discomfort as part of the trip, but an incident with the passenger had annoyed him.

The man coughed. "Sir, the dust is getting in my nose! I'm going to step outside a moment before the coach takes off."

Before the passenger could step out the door, the judge said, "How do you do, sir? I'm Judge Thomas Mackey, going to Abbeville to try a murder case. What's your name and what do you do?"

The man was tall, slender and outwardly nervous. He found the stage and its movement uncomfortable as it departed the station. He finally settled down and said, "Nice to meet you. I am a jeweler going to my new job in Greenville. Name's Bertrum Lambert." He offered his hand, giving a friendly shake to the judge.

"Do you have any hobbies, Bertrum?"

"No, sir."

"Why not?"

"My time was taken up, for I was learning my skill," said Bertrum.

"Never got around to it, I'll bet! Well, sir, let me tell you about mine. I am experimenting with bees and lightning bugs," announced the judge.

"Good heavens! Why?" said the man.

"Why? It's a wonderful idea! If I am successful in crossing them, the bees will be able to find their hives at night and all sorts of things. Don't you know! If I can get them to mate, it'll be a great discovery. I've been working on this for quite some time."

"Really, I must sit by the other window. Oh, my, bees and lightning bugs! Oh, my!" said Bertrum concealing his mouth with his hand.

Mackey tried to explain his theory, but the man's lack of knowledge and interest perturbed the judge. He could say no more, for the man covered his ears and would not listen.

"Some people don't know anything. Educated people are so hard to find these days," said the judge. He decided to head for the drug store, where a special place to sit and chat was always available to him and friends who listened to his every word.

He stayed in town many times. When he passed the houses and stores, the citizens greeted him. He longed to speak to anyone who would listen to his language, clothed in legal textbook information and committed to memory. He prided himself on this fact. His eyes glistened as he watched in anticipation for a person's reaction to the words and ideas that flowed from his mouth. Friends who listened received advice for their sons and daughters to follow in their growing years.

He bragged about serving as captain in Sterling Price's army, and, also in the senate during Reconstruction.

When he arrived at the drug store, he noticed a big sign on the door advertising "fresh drugs." The notice said the store received new paints, oils, tobacco, brandies, wines, stationery, and confections every month, cheap for cash. "Come in and see for yourselves."

This enticed the judge, and he went in.

"Hey there, judge," said Foley, the proprietor, trying to get his one arm in his suit coat. "Sure glad to see you."

Two other men hurried to shake the judge's hand.

Foley tipped the chair and his friend, Gaylord, moved. "Sit here, judge. This chair's got a pillow," said Foley.

The men huddled closer in their chairs to his honor as if they were favored.

"Gentlemen, how have things been?" said Mackey, confident he would be advised of all the news.

"There's been a murder at the Franklins. That's all the town's been talkin' about," said Foley. "What ya gonna do about it? David's as guilty as sin."

"Now, Foley, you know I can't divulge the case just yet, but you know I love South Carolina, sir. It's in my blood. She gave birth to twins, one white and one black. Therefore, I always have a plan, and it will surely make him confess to this terrible deed."

"Judge! Ah'll be at the trial waitin' and watchin'."

Another man named Conway grabbed his suspenders with his thumbs, pushed his chair back and said, "Ah got some news." Everyone looked at him. When he was sure of their attention, Conway continued. "Heard it at Turner's store last week."

"What's so important?" said Gaylord, putting his feet up on the table. Everyone quieted and listened.

"Gideon O'Neil come into some money found in the Franklin cabin."

"We know that," said Foley.

"Do you know he's gonna buy a new farm, maybe bigger like Fulton's?" said Gaylord, proudly divulging what he kept secret for several days. "He was looking for one." He paused and added, "Truthfully, he ain't much of a farmer."

"Well, he darn right thinks he is," said Foley.

"Oh, judge," said Gaylord. "Bob Nickels is back. Gone a long time carin' for his mother in Tennessee. Guess she died an' he come back. Lotta work on his farm. Heard his wife cried when she saw the old place. A lot o' work when you leave it a long time."

"Don't recall him," said Mackey.

"Keeps to himself mostly," said Conway. "Lives near the Franklins. He was in Tennessee, so no use in puttin' him under suspicion."

"Well, I suspect a lot," said Mackey. "Got one in jail under prime suspicion now and just as sure as anything, there'll be a confession."

"That's it, judge," said the men.

"Yes, as I believe in my experiment involving lightning bugs and bees, there'll be a confession."

"Lightning bugs and bees?" said Foley.

"Let me tell you about it," said the judge.

*　*　*　*　*

The February chill continued to encompass the crowded courtroom, and Jim put a large shawl over his shoulders. He looked at Jeff. People were still making noise and talking, so Jim thought it was a good time to speak to his client.

"How are you feeling? Like your strength is gone?" said Jim to Jeff, who looked down most of the time.

"Yes, suh, my stomach goes round and round."

"Jeff, I am trying to do you justice. Your case was thrust upon me without a great deal of preparation."

"Ah understands, Massa Jim. You do the best you can."

Jim desperately wanted to try harder for his client and win the all-male jury over to Jeff's side. The pervasive feeling in the courtroom and the evidence already presented against the dark-skinned man made Jim's job worrisome to him. He knew the evidence about the yellow stain found on the knife in the bushes on the Franklin property. Others claimed it was found in Jeff's pocket, with the yellow stain on it. He hoped this did not convince the jury of Jeff's guilt.

"Mr. O'Neil," said Jim, as the trial began, "you are sure of the stain on this knife. I don't want there to be any doubt in your mind. Look closely and carefully."

"Jim, you know I looked and looked. Yes, the stain on the knife is from the persimmon bush. It's a special stain. Seen it many times."

"Your honor, I need to confer with my client for a moment," asked Jim.

Permission was granted and Jim said to Jeff, "We'll keep Gideon on the stand. I'll continue questioning him about your relationship with the Franklins, which I'm sure was good."

Jeff nodded. Jim felt nothing could be said, for he knew the verdict was already pronounced, but he wanted to make one last attempt at something good. After the preliminaries, Jim asked Gideon, "Mr. O'Neil, how long have the Davids been with the Franklin family?"

"Why, uh, many years. Even 'fore the war. Aunt Drusilla took Mandy, Jeff's woman, with them when they come from Charleston and picked up Jeff in Columbia when they come to settle at the springs."

"You agree, Mr. O'Neil, that the Davids have served the Franklins for many years."

"Rightly so, but that don't stop nobody from murderin'."

The thunderous applause and shouting of "good answer back" and "that's tellin' em" was all in the witness's favor.

Judge Mackey pounded his gavel many times, demanding order. When silence fell at last and the court was restored to order, Jim reiterated his statement.

"Mr. O'Neil, the point concerned the length of service the Davids had with the Franklins, not your pronouncement of guilt. Tell the court, to your knowledge did Jeff do his assigned tasks daily?"

"Yes, suh."

"Did he ever fail to appear for work?" Gideon shook his head.

"Was he willing to work hard and not complain?"

"Yes, suh, he worked hard. Uncle George never said nothin' 'bout his complainin'."

"Jeff was also entrusted with the money from the crops sold in town. Do you know of any proof to show that Jeff did not return the acquired amount to Miss Drusilla at any time?"

"No, suh, I don't."

"Was Jeff ever paid in cash for his services?"

"Vera little, I 'spect. Most pay was food an' a place to live an' clothes on their backs."

"Jeff had very little if any money of his own."

"He didn' go nowhere. He didn' need money."

"How did the Franklins show their respect for the Davids?"

"Respect! Hmmm, they jus' all got along. Not much spoken 'tween them at times, but they jus' all got along. Besides, Jeff and family worked for mah aunt and uncle."

"The court can safely assume since there was no quarrel between the parties, Jeff worked hard as the 'palm of a plough-man.' In other words, he had the hands of a hard worker for many years and had little money if any, never complaining. The

Franklins trusted him. Tell the court, Gideon, if there was ever a cross word between Jeff David and your aunt and uncle on your visits to their cabin."

Gideon was restless, but the judge gave him reassuring glances. The crowd waited pensively.

Jim closed his eyes. He barely moved his lips and pleaded, "Oh heaven, please be truthful and have Gideon answer this carefully." After a few seconds, he repeated the question.

Gideon wiggled in his chair and scowled a bit. He appeared to be thinking his reply over carefully. He shook his head, "No suh."

This was the sweetest sound Jim hoped to hear. He loudly exclaimed, "You are testifying that you never heard a cross word between the Franklins and the Davids upon your many visitations to the Franklin farm."

"Yes, suh. No cross words, but that don' stop a murder for money!"

Again, the spectators shouted and clapped their approval. The judge pounded his gavel until order was restored. O'Neil stepped down, straightening his tie and smiling all the way to his seat, enjoying the attention. The next witness called and sworn in was none other than James King, dressed in a brand new suit. He proudly took the stand like a celebrity, viewing the audience, making sure all eyes were on him. A few of the young women swooned and whispered about the fact that he never married.

Jim asked King some related questions about the murder, but King wanted to take credit for finding Jeff's footprints. Jim turned the questioning to the subject.

"Where did you find Jeff's footprints?" he inquired.

"I found them on a narrow path leading away from the

cabin to the spot where the persimmon club was cut and back to the cabin."

"Tell the court how you can be sure they were Jeff's footprints?"

"Why, sir, his foot fit right into them." The spectators applauded.

"Order. Order in the court," shouted the judge pounding his gavel.

King continued by brushing a fleck from his coat. "After he was arrested, and before he was taken away, I went to the spot and showed the crowd just where his foot fit in. I swear those are Jeff's footprints leading away from the Franklin cabin."

Since Jim had not been to the cabin, he could not think of anything else except that he was told there were many people at the cabin that morning after the murder, trampling all around. How Jeff's footprints were singled out was a mystery.

Judah, the last witness, reinforced everything King stated and twitched his black beard, which made the spectators laugh. He too declared Jeff guilty and testified wholeheartedly against him even accusing Jeff of getting away without him to bring the coroner from Greenwood.

"That proves him guilty. He wanted to run away. Jeff wasn't suppos'd to leave without me. Ah had to move fast to catch up with him," stated Judah.

"Were you on a horse, Judah?" said Jim.

"Yeah, an' Jeff walked beside me. After all, I sure couldn't let him escape since he was under suspicion. We all come back in the doc's wagon."

There was a pause. Jim turned and said, "Judah, how did you know Jeff was under suspicion?"

"Everyone kept an eye on him. He didn't look right at people."

"This witness can step down, your honor. No further questions."

Judah said, "I wanna add a last statement."

"Questioning is over, your honor. The witness may step down now!" replied Jim.

Jim's opportunity came to address the jury. He felt for his client. He wished he had done better for Jeff. The faces of the men were serious. They frowned at Jim, while some of the jurors seemed to shake their heads. Jim tried to appear confident approaching the box. He stepped forward ready to begin his presentation, no matter what might happen.

"Gentlemen, let's look at the facts and not be so willing to pronounce sentence before reason. The robber or robbers were of the same mind. The Franklins had money hidden. The robbers decided to rip the cabin apart to find it. Remember, Jeff had no money. His cabin was searched after he went to jail. There was no money anywhere. No evidence or testimony presented in this case showed that Jeff had any money.

"Remember, he worked hard for the Franklins. They had a good relationship with each other. They trusted Jeff with returning any money from selling the wares at the market."

Jim stepped back from the box and faced the spectators in the courtroom. In a moment, he composed himself and turned back to the jurors.

"Keep this in mind. Jeff gave faithful service in return and no complaints regarding his conduct from anyone were ever presented. It's plain the murders were committed for money purposes. It is a fact that George and Drusilla could definitely have secretly accumulated and hidden $11,000 in their humble abode. Only $5,000 was recovered, scattered about the cabin after the murderer or murderers left. One skirt in Drusilla's room that the robbers overlooked had two hundred dollars sewn in the lining."

The crowd gasped and went into a loud conversation. The judge tried to maintain order. One woman who was hard of hearing reported to her friend, "Drusilla had $400 dollars sewn in her skirt. Think what we could do with $400."

Jim continued when the judge quieted the court.

"You could ask yourselves, why didn't Jeff pick this up? That's right. He had no money. The Franklins were good to Jeff and his family. He did not commit this murder. The evidence is weak."

Jim called for a motion for a new trial. He argued and pleaded for one by saying, "May I remind the court, the prisoners did come to trial on their lack of knowledge for counsel. I, knowing very little of this case, had been appointed by the court to defend the Davids. I feel sure in time I will find evidence favorable to Jeff."

Silence ruled the courtroom. Judge Mackey sat smugly in his chair. He leaned forward and said, "The motion for a new trial is refused. Jeff David shall receive the death sentence."

The court was in an uproar! People shouted and jumped. The judge pounded his gavel and had the clerk clear the room.

"I'm sorry, Jeff. Honestly!" said Jim. He saw the old man taken out of court and his heart grieved for him. Jim believed Jeff was innocent. Deep in his heart the attorney knew that nothing more could be done. Judge Mackey's instructions to the jury and his rulings during the trial were all unobjectionable and absolutely left no grounds for appeal to the highest court.

A few days later, Jim walked through the corridor of the courthouse concentrating on some important papers. He held them tightly in his hands. He was tired from the extended workload and longed to be home in peace and quiet with Lauren. He realized he didn't look where he was going and became startled when he saw a figure running down the hall after him, waving a sheet of paper.

Jim saw James and under his breath he said, "Oh, Lord, what does he want?" Jim could not imagine.

"Jim, Jim, I'm glad I found you. Your clerk had me looking all over. Afraid I'm a bit breathless, but I wanted to find you." James took off his hat. "It would please me if you would sign this paper." He slipped it out of his pocket and handed it to Jim.

Suspicion came over Jim because of the captains' polite tone of voice and his deliberate manner of doing so. He stood there and grinned at Jim, who did not acknowledge James in anyway. What was this paper and why was it so important? Jim took the paper and opened it with care not to tear its binding. He started to read it and said, "What can I do, James?"

"Jim, you know what the document is. It's the reward for the conviction of old Jeff…a petition to Governor Wade Hampton to pay the reward to Judah and me."

"A reward!" replied the attorney, shocked and confused.

"Yes, Jim, see this line?" James showed him with his finger. "There's two rewards. The governor offered $250, and O'Neil and the other Franklin relatives, $500."

"Seven hundred and fifty dollars!" exclaimed Jim.

"Why, Jim," said James, apparently astounded at the attorney's remark. Jim frowned as James continued speaking. "The judge, the solicitor and all the jury members signed the petition. I hope you won't object to signing it."

Jim breathed deeply and felt the anger build up within. It took all the strength he could muster to remember who he was and what his position meant to reply as calmly as he could. "James, this is indeed shocking news to me!"

"Jim, it's the best and most legal document under the circumstances," said James, perturbed at Jim's attitude.

"Hear me well," said Jim, hoping he had his temper under control. "I absolutely will not sign your petition. I had not been informed or notified of any rewards. If I had, Jeff would not have been convicted. Believe me when I tell you that now he will not be hanged. You and the others will not get your money! And, if I may add, your politeness is a bit overdone."

The men stared at each other angrily. The beady eyes of the captain glared in dissatisfaction and disgust.

Jim felt that his face was flushed, but he stood firm in his convictions, even though James tried desperately once again to change Jim's mind. "You know, Jim, Jeff was found guilty, and he had a fair trial. You also know there was nothing more to do. Everyone, including Judge Mackey did the right thing."

Jim looked at James in disdain. He thought of the character patterns of both men, King and Arnold. Jim believed they were lacking courage but always bragging about their escapades. Both men could easily have taken a bribe to testify falsely against Jeff. Since when were they ever friends?

Jim still had the paper in his hand. Before James, he crushed the petition and threw the paper on the floor. Jim walked away, leaving the captain to stand alone with everyone looking at him.

In less than an hour, Jim sent his office clerk to inform Lauren that he was investigating the David case and would not be home for a few days.

CHAPTER 10

After a hearty breakfast, Jim and Frank stood outside in the pre-dawn darkness, waiting for their horses. Frank rubbed his hands together and said, "Chillier this morning, isn't it?"

"Yes, I am a bit chilled too," said Jim who paced up and down.

"What is taking the stable boy so long? I informed him last night before we retired."

Jim knew the trip to the Franklin property was necessary to secure the details and information for the court case, and he also knew it would be difficult for Frank because of information that might be found.

"Frank, you're not nervous about going again, are you?" said Jim, folding his arms this time and keeping an eye out for any reaction Frank may have.

"No, what makes you say that?"

"Well, it's been my experience that people get excited and scared returning to the scene of the crime. The first time they don't know what to expect, and they follow through with whatever happens, but the second time they know exactly what occurred and are conditioned to it."

"Jim, you make such profound statements. I don't feel nervous, if that is what you mean. I...I don't feel much of anything. I haven't talked to either Franklin for years, and you know the story about that one. I…I don't know what else to say."

The problem, Jim thought, *is facts. Frank has got to be sure of the facts. Maybe returning to the Franklins will straighten out the situation.* In Jim's heart, he really did not suspect Frank as being one of the murderers, but then again, Frank may have made some blunders in his own search for the truth, and Jim was anxious to ask him, when the time was right, why he didn't appear in court. He would ask Bob too. How much easier this case could have been on Jeff if Jim had known the facts first hand. Frank had been a resident of the area a long time. He knew what to expect of its people and circumstances. *His not coming to the trial is cowardly,* thought Jim.

"How did Bob react as both of you inspected the Franklin grounds?" said Jim.

"Oh, he did all right. He was there before I was and walked around as much as he could waiting for someone to go in the cabin with him."

"Bob is honest and does not lose faith in life with all its problems," said Jim. "I sure hope, since the two of you were on the scene, that answers to my questions will be forthcoming. I truly need all and any information I can get to save Jeff."

"You truly believe the black man innocent, don't you?" said Frank.

Jim eyed him with disbelief at what he just heard. Didn't Frank believe Jeff also, even after what he said at his house? Jim thought. Then he replied, "His word is as good as your help, and you believe your help, don't you?"

"Where's those horses? It's been too long. Boy! Boy! Hurry up! Hurry up!" shouted Frank.

As Jim and Frank kept the horses gait at a steady pace,

Frank counted the minutes it took to reach their destination. He knew they were almost to the murder location when Jim noticed the sky changing to gray. Jim looked up at the dark sky, thinking it would probably rain before the day ended.

"Let's get to the Franklin place before any outdoor evidence is washed away in case it rains," said Jim hurriedly to Frank.

When they came upon Indigo Springs and Simms Crossroads, Bob waved to them. He too apparently felt a chill in his hands and feet and walked around to keep warm. The men greeted each other and approached the premises carefully. Jim hurried ahead, hoping to discover anything that would help him in Jeff's behalf.

"Come on, gentlemen, time's a'wasting before the rain."

"I got some ideas in mind, Jim," said Bob. "I don't know where you want to start, though. Say Frank, are you nervous? You seem rather tense."

"You know what I have to go through here."

Bob nodded and said to Frank, "Believe in yourself first."

Of course, Jim's curiosity and anxiousness led the men forward. He looked around the grounds as carefully as he could, walking toward the cabin. Jim was not surprised at what he saw. The yard remained in disarray, as if a terrible wind had engulfed it. Paper, boxes, pieces of food, sticks and holes dug by children had dispersed themselves in various places all over the property.

When the men were a hundred yards from the house, Frank broke the silence and pointed to the sandbank where King and Arnold swore the tracks were Jeff's.

"This is what I tried to explain," said Jim. "See where the path leads from the cabin to the big road? All those footprints."

"That's true," said Bob to Jim. "Everyone tramped around the day of the murder before King and Arnold came. Long before the crowd came, Frank and I walked along the path and crossed the ditch. We didn't see one track."

Jim said, "All right, that's understood, but let's check the stump of the persimmon sapling cut by the murderer or murderers and used as the club to kill the Franklins."

Jim's special reason for wanting to inquire about this part of the investigation as soon as possible remained deep inside him and evident to him alone. He knew this part would be difficult for Frank. Without any discussion about it immediately, the case could not be solved.

The two men led Jim about 20 yards into the wooded area in back of the Franklin property. Persimmon bushes, pines, some raspberry and thistle-like foliage grew there. The persimmon saplings grew clustered together. The three men just stood for a minute and eyed the group of bushes. Frank hesitated while Bob and Jim watched him pensively, waiting for Frank's next move. Jim was aware of the difficult task the captain faced. With lightening speed, Frank grabbed hold of a branch with his only hand. The top part had been cut off at the height of his shoulder.

"Jim," said Frank seriously, with tears in his eyes. "There is no doubt in my mind that the club used on the Franklins was cut from this sapling. Look and study the size and the knife marks on it. Also, when you go in the wooded area, there were men's tracks as plain as day leading toward the cabin. You'd never have known that till now."

"Frank, you know I believe you," said Jim.

His friend's eyes filled with tears. "You must know, Jim, if

Bob and I…if the crowd knew…if anyone knew about the cutting of the club, they would have arrested me for murder. That's what scares the hell out of me. Bob knows this, for I'd be in Jeff's predicament or worse. They could have hung me on the spot the way the crowd reacted in their swayed thinking."

"It is obvious," said Jim, "the club was cut by a one-armed man about Frank's height. We all know that he too has no left hand to help him, for by the knife marks, it was cut by the right hand."

"Jim," said Frank, "I am very nervous over this." He bent over as though he were going to fall. "It makes me sick. I think I am going to throw up. I've got to sit down, or maybe I'll faint. What should be done?"

"I am sick too, sick of a lot of things, people and attitudes. My job though is to clear Jeff of murder, and I suggest we never mention a name I am sure we have in mind. Agreed?"

"Makes sense in this case, even though it pains us," said Bob.

Jim understood the evidence as it was presented, and he fully realized how painfully difficult this summation appeared to Frank. After some discussion and another evaluation of the evidence, Bob said, "A person trying to cut a limb of this nature needs something to hold it steady so the limb won't bend or snap up."

Jim asserted, "Men with two arms would hold one end of the sapling against the force of the right hand, but a one-armed man couldn't cut it. He would cut only at his shoulder or knee. That part of the body would press against the force of the cutting, and if he's lucky, he won't injure himself while doing it."

Frank stressed, "A person can break the branch, twist it into ribbons and run a knife through those ribbons. He can cut deeper and farther at the shoulder than the knee."

"Look," said Bob, "you can see the one-armed murderer cut this at the shoulder height till it was about two-thirds cut open, and my shoulder is shorter, as you can surely observe."

"That's what I told you last night, Jim," said Frank.

Bob said, "Jim, I figure the one-armed man must have turned his back and broke the club off over his shoulder, pulling the sapling back and forth until the uncut part was in ribbons."

"Yes, yes, that's it," said Jim. "I believe we are hitting on something!" He clapped his hands. "By golly, let's examine the knife marks now that appear on the ribbons."

"Note these," said Bob, "the other saplings over here." He leaned toward the ground where the murderer tried to cut the club at his shoulder. "These show he tried to cut a couple loose at this knee."

The secret circumstances long shrouded in a veil of mystery became lifted for Jim, who studied the situation and asked a number of questions.

"See," interjected Frank. "The person cut at the height of my knee, cutting about half-way through, but found he could not cut deeper at the knee."

By this time, Frank was feeling sick inside and emotionally upset. He tried to break the branch on his knee, but the roots popped up, startling him.

"I feel bad, gentlemen. The reality of this situation hit me harder than Christmas Day," said Frank. "I can't keep on with this. I've got to leave here."

Jim grabbed Frank tightly by his arm, in case he fell from the forces of the branches snapping back, and moved him away.

"Here the murderer must have finally succeeded in cutting the other sapling used as the club, the murderer's club." The men looked at Frank with concern.

"Frank, we know you did not do this terrible deed. You have other things to think about. We know you must feel lost and alone. You have the farm you love, you have children and a family. There's no reason for you to hate. Knowing someone for a long time, and then finding out the worst in a person leaves you defeated and without a victory or belief."

"If you don't need me for anything," said Frank rubbing his hand, "I'm heading to my farm. It's a refuge and strength for me there."

"Sure, Bob and I understand," said Jim. "I hope both of you are aware how hurtful this is for me too, especially when I think of the past and my coming here. I think of happier times, and no matter what happens to us or to him, may the best be there for everyone, no matter what. This almost makes me speechless thinking about it."

Frank looked at the men. "If the conclusion you've drawn in your minds as to the murderer is the same as mine, then we, as friends feel the loss of a bond we one had, a kin to us. It astounds me that I knew this person, shared his joys and sorrows, fought side by side with him, and watched him deteriorate into behavior patterns no one understands. It puzzles me. To hear after all these years he took part in degradation and murder, his situation is worse than sin," answered Frank.

"You can't live his life for him, Frank. He made his choices. Maybe even a long time ago," said Jim. "It's unfortunate. We all change. That's what I tried to tell you concerning the railroad. We've got to change, ourselves and the community."

Frank looked up at Jim and said, "It's up to you now and what to do."

"I know. It's the fate of an innocent man that upsets me most! Your attention and help here go far more than any thanks."

"What will you do, Jim?" said Frank.

"Frank, I don't know what to say or do right now myself. Truthfully, I never expected this at any time," said Jim. "When I first saw the club in the courtroom, I had no inkling of who or what could have done this. It's so bizarre. Why?"

The men stood speechless. No one could say anything. They never suspected the murderer to be someone they knew. Jim felt determined to free Jeff but had for the moment lost his commitment to this cause. He knew anything he said would have a profound affect on the men. He wanted to speak as a friend to both of them. "You know, gentlemen, as I stand here now and perceive what I understand about this case, it never ceases to amaze me how mankind reacts to external forces over which they believe they have no control. What will I do? I will take one step at a time until I have taken all the steps."

"He cannot be tried, can he?" questioned Bob. "Why, it would kill the people who love him."

"The question may not be about a trial, but who will defend him?" said Jim.

"Jim!" shouted Frank going over to Jim and grabbing him by the collar. "You can't mean that."

Jim put his hands on top of Frank's and said, "I certainly do."

They looked each other. Bob took a step to defend Jim. He said, "Let's think this over. Jim has a case and evidence to prove a man innocent. Let him do that first."

Frank let his hands go and walked away. He departed on horseback. His only farewell was a salute to the men who watched him ride away. Jim thought this was the end of a long friendship, but he knew he could not defend Sam should it come to that.

Bob watched Frank disappear into the distance. "I never saw a man so disappointed and emotionally hurt from this experience. I did not know what to do or what to say. Sort of thought he would get over it, but I knew it would not be true since he didn't appear at the trial, and Jim...I was afraid to say anything."

"We best not mention the name...ever," said Jim solemnly.

"Before anyone came to the cabin, Frank swore he'd report all about the murder and what happened, but did nothing, just remained quiet and pensive. When the men tried to hang Jeff, he backed off. Those people were tough. They only had one thing in mind and grabbed for Jeff. I was worried. They listened to no one."

Jim sat down on a stump. He put his head in his hands and rested for a moment before answering. "Bob, in some ways, I am not totally surprised when I think of past events. But thank goodness, he left the murder scene when he did, or Frank would be in jail too. If anyone discovered the bush and thought of a one-armed man with him standing right there, I dread to think of the consequences. So, let's get on with it."

"I dread to think of it too, Jim. Let's get over toward the house. I want to show you something we overlooked before in the front yard."

As he walked over to the spot, Bob added, "I found two half-burnt sperm candles in the front yard." He took them from his pocket and gave them to Jim. "The situation is like this, that at the first cabin inspection, no such candles were found, but because the Franklins used only the home-made tallow type, Frank and I noticed one such candle had burned to its socket in a dish on the supper table. I saw the sperm candles in Turner's store."

"Bob, I am astounded that nothing of this nature was mentioned at the trial."

"Then it is imperative I tell you this too. Frank and I found the murderer's club a few feet from the candles. From the front yard, tracks were found leading to the pig-pens. No hogs had been in them for awhile. The pens were broken, as though someone in the dark blundered into them."

Bob also showed Jim the footprints, that he and Frank covered up because of the crowd leading toward the plowed field.

"I want to tell you," said Bob, "two sets of footprints—one set was large, the other smaller. Frank and I thought these footprints were of a companion, Maybe a black man and a white man. We traced the tracks across the field. From the length of the steps, I'd say that the men must have been running."

The prints stopped at the dead pine tree at the edge of the woods just outside the fence. The men continued searching cautiously.

"Look," said Jim. "Farther down the road here is where a horse could have been hitched to this fence. The man with the smaller feet mounted it. See the print?"

"Then the other accomplice must have walked beside him towards Greenwood and parted at the fork in the road. There the man on horseback turned to the right. The road leads to Greenville after about 50 miles."

"So, he's gone!" muttered Jim.

The two men hurried back to the place where the horse had been hitched, looking for more tracks. "We'll have to look hard," said Jim. "Much time has gone by."

They searched the ground as thoroughly as they could. In fact, Jim felt his own life depended on it. After many minutes passed, Jim shouted, "Luck is with us. Look here. After all this time here are footprints leading from the dead tree to the rail fence on the upper side of the field."

"Why sure. We must be doing something right. Christmas Eve was a clear night. In fact, no one could help watching the moon. It was so bright," said Bob.

'Yes," said Jim. "The men could have easily hidden behind the pokeberry bushes at the fence corner. The robbers must have waited until they saw a flicker of candlelight in the one back window. See? The steps leading away were made in haste."

"The incoming steps are shorter and irregular. Probably the companion snuck close to the cabin to peek in the rear window," said his friend.

The men agreed that the intruders may have waited until they were sure the Franklins had sat down to eat their thrifty meal on the small supper table.

"God! I can't believe none of this was mentioned at the trial," said Jim. "Neither of you were summoned to testify. The testimony of King and Arnold concerning the tracks was relied upon too heavily by the State's solicitor. Let's go over everything carefully of what I know now from you and Frank. I need to be sure I understand every detail," said Jim.

The lawyer and his friend discussed everything that happened in full perspective and detail, trying not to miss a point. If they thought anything related to the case would be talk, gossip or hearsay, Jim dismissed it as such. In his mind, the suspected the murderer could be none other than Sam Turner. Sam lived in many places, stayed away from home for long periods of time, and became desperate for attention these last several months, and his behavior became questionable to Jim and others. Since Tom's mysterious death and burial, people gossiped about the money arguments Tom and Sam were known to have. After the Randolph killing, it was noted that the men came into a lot of money by mysterious circumstances. Then a short time later, Tom was dead.

"Jim, this question is burning in my mind. I've got to ask it, and I won't say the name. Will you answer this inquiry? Where is he? Do you know? It's just the two of us here, and I am really wondering where he is or where could he have gone."

"All I know is the sheriff got to Tom's funeral too late and could not find Sam's traces anywhere. A small posse looked for him for days, but without luck."

As Jim and Bob silently walked to their horses, Jim began to reminisce about Sam and Frank.

"You know, Bob, before we draw any conclusions, maybe it is fitting to tell you how Sam and Frank served in the war together. Turner was the one who saved Fuller's life, and Sam lost his arm. Later, of course, Frank lost his through an accident. So, perhaps that bond kept them together and then tore them apart. It's funny. When Sam felt like a friendly chat, he communicated just how he saved Frank's life, usually exaggerating as the year passed. But his conversation ended on a bitter tone when Frank became the prosperous one."

"Thanks for telling me, Jim. I never realized they were that close. I had to go to Tennessee and lost ties with the area. Guess

I knew I'd always come back 'cause me and my wife love the folks here."

"The day is passing fast. Let's head over to Doc Waddell's and confirm some of these statements with him, especially about when he examined the bodies."

A brief rain shower struck as they arrived at the doctor's home. The men sat inside the warm room and listened to the doctor, who spoke freely.

Doc Waddell leaned back in his chair and put his legs on a stool. Doc Waddell stretched and said, "Yes, it's a terrible thing, but George received an extremely heavy blow, hard enough to topple any man over, and repeated blows broke his skull. On Miss Drusilla's left temple, one of the heavy blows made a gash that must have bled profusely. I determined earlier that she could have fallen beside a chair for a time after the blow was administered because on the floor was a small pool of blood with gray hairs stuck to it. While she lay there, her head could have moved back and forth."

"As I understand it, Doc, she was found in her bedroom," replied Jim.

"Yes. Wait. While her head moved back and forth, the bleeding could have cleared her brain, restoring her senses. Jim, it's highly probable to me that while she was in her unconscious state, the robbers searched the room thoroughly with a vengeance, looking for all the money they could find," answered Doc Waddell.

"All right," said Bob. "How do you figure she got to the bedroom?"

The doc scratched his chin. He took a deep breath and sunk back further in his chair. He thought a moment more and said,

"I suspect she struggled to her feet somehow...must have been something going on in her little room."

"That's right," said Jim. "Sure, that explains the sperm candles. She could have been startled by a light in her room. The robbers must have used a candle."

"Sure thing," said Bob. "That's where we found the fur-covered chest. Must have been her treasure."

Jim agreed. "Instincts would have, of course, forced her to guard her money. Especially a woman of her caliber. It's possible she even recognized one of the men."

"My sentiments exactly," said Doc.

"There are still questions remaining. For instance, I keep asking myself over and over: Did the thieves intend to knock the victims unconscious for the time it took to find the money? Or, was the murder committed to keep all this a secret?" asked Jim.

Bob and the Doc shrugged their shoulders and shook their heads. They couldn't answer the questions.

"Jim, don't you think that explains why Drusilla's body was half on the bed?" asked Bob.

The doctor spoke first, "Yes, but remember, she was struck in the left temple, and the way she fell on the bed face down with her feet in the floor could have put her in that position. The blows to George's head and his sister's were sufficient enough to cause unconsciousness but not to kill."

"It seems to me that the first blows could have been struck when the door first opened," Jim said.

"Yes," said Doc, "George's back was right at the door and his sister's was facing him at the end of the small table by the chair."

"I'm going to conclude," said Jim, "that the first blows were the work of the companion, who I'll assume was black because the other man could not take a chance on being recognized."

I'll add this since I was the first man there, that whoever they are searched for money. Everything was ransacked. The sperm candles were lit, too. George's pockets were turned inside out. The criminals seemed to be in no hurry because the place was dark and secluded."

"That gave the intruders a chance to discover some money," said Jim. "At finding more of it, the greedy men were gleefully anticipating riches in the thousands of dollars. Then, someone or something stopped them from completely uncovering the contents of the fur-covered chest."

"In haste they ran from the cabin, probably hitting Drusilla once more. Because they hurried, they threw things away and rammed into the pigpens. This way they could head in the direction of the plowed field," said Bob.

"Gentlemen," said Jim, "I believe the murders were committed to conceal the crime. When the robbers saw poor old Drusilla, her thin frame, staggering, with her head all bloody, she must have been a spectacle. She definitely saw someone she knew, and it all ended in the horrible murders of two old people."

"If there is no more discussion, I see my wife signaling me from then other room. Guess there's a patient or two to see right now. Thanks for coming, gentlemen, and good luck, Jim. I feel better now that it really is in your hands," said the doctor, and left the room.

A short time later, Jim and Bob rode past the Franklin place again. They went into the yard and checked where the murderer's club had been thrown. Jim wanted to assure himself that the murders had not been committed when the white man and black man entered the cabin, for there would not have been further use of the club. The club would not be in the hands of the men when they fled.

Fundamentally, Jim was satisfied, but he anticipated that the long road ahead of him to clear Jeff would be a troublesome path.

During the time Jim and Bob sought clues and information about the murders, Frank rode weary and broken-hearted toward the narrow, winding road that would take him to his door. His head was down and he felt tired, alone, and depressed at what had happened. Disappointed too over Jim's implication that he would not defend Sam, Frank became teary-eyed. He asked himself, *what has become of kinship, a closeness, comradeship in people? At first, we helped each other, offered support and strength, trusted, loaned money, protected reputations, loved like a brother, and then, when some situation comes about that is not related to the other person's liking, he deserts the very people that he wants to help, forgetting all ties that bind one person to another and people to people. Kinship...it's all gone like the dead in a war!*

CHAPTER 11

Lauren, restless and lonely, finished her sewing and put it down on the table next to her chair. As the evening darkness descended, she felt more aware of Jim being gone.

She was the only person in the room. *I feel scared,* she thought. *I know I'm not a brave person. I don't know what to do with myself. My maid keeps asking questions and puts ideas in my head that make me wonder, and the cook goes to bed early. I'm at a loss.*

She wrung her hands and wished for Jim. *When he's here, we talk over the day, and he lets me in on some of the cases. No names, of course, but his being here means so much to me. Now, I've got to be a woman, a brave woman. I've got to be what he expects of me,* she thought.

Her supper was brought in by the cook, who looked at her sternly, as though she knew it would be one of those nights again where Lauren could not sleep without Jim. She ate very little of her supper, even though the cook placed her tray attractively near the fireplace with a big napkin, silver dishes and flowers. Afterward, in search of something to do to pass the time, she wandered around the upstairs till she found Jim's textbooks in the desk drawer and began reading in the places he had marked. Lauren liked to be informed about Jim's studies and the cases he carried. This gave her a confidence in her husband's work but made her wonder how Jim kept up with the tasks involving his work.

She sat down in his big desk chair and thought of his ambition to be a good attorney, with the underlying objective to become a judge someday, when the opportunity presented itself. If he could have helped Jeff sooner, the possibility of a judgeship might have been open to him.

"Anyway, I do think about how he is making out," said Lauren out loud. "I hope Frank will be able to assist Jim in his endeavors to aid Jeff." She shook her head and mumbled, "He was very depressed when the guilty verdict was passed."

She moaned in boredom, sat back in the chair and dozed off, holding the book on her lap.

As the clock struck 10, Lauren awoke surprised by a knock at her door.

"It's me, Miz Lauren, Miranda. I comes to help you in bed," said the maid, who opened the door quietly. She came in swinging her apron and fingering her curls under her cap. Miranda, a petite, lighter skinned girl about 18, was pretty, slender of figure, and confident of her surroundings.

"Why, what time is it? I must have slept," said Lauren, smoothing her dress.

"Ten o'clock."

"Good heavens, it's late. What are you doing up so late?"

"Sittin' by the fire and thinkin'. Time jus' went by, Miz Lauren. Cook went to sleep early, but I'm thinkin'."

"Thinking about what, Miranda?"

"Well, poor ol' Mr. Jeff. Wonderin' what he's doin' and where he'll end up. Mr. Jim was sick a couple days, Miz Lauren."

"Be positive, Miranda. Mr. Benet is on the case, and he's finding more evidence in Jeff's favor. Pray too. Believe me, that helps a lot. Now, fix my bed."

"Yes, ma'm."

The maid pulled out a favorite gown and fussed over Lauren's pillows, fluffing them into big balloons.

"Don't forget to secure all the doors, Miranda, when my husband is away. You can sleep on the couch downstairs," said Lauren.

"Yes, ma'm, and I won't forgets to light the small candles in the window downstair."

"Yes, and one up here. I don't like the dark."

"I knows. It's best to have a warm body right next to you. Right, Miz Lauren?"

Lauren did not answer Miranda. She did not like her implication but said, "I'll put out the candle near the morning. I know I'll be awake."

"Yes, ma'm. This night be so quiet," said Miranda. She helped Lauren off with her dress and pulled the pins out of Lauren's silky, long, brown hair.

The maid spoke as she tucked Lauren in bed. "Miz Lauren, I comes to ask you a question."

"Yes, what is it?"

"Ma'm, I hears Jeff is not supposed to ask for anything. I know he's got stomach pains an' he asks for some soup. The jailer didn' give him any. He asks for Mr. Jim too. He's gone an' can't come. What should Jeff be doin'? Please, Miz Lauren, tell me!"

"I heard his wife is allowed to bring him his food. Now ease your mind about that. If it will make you feel better, have Cook take him some soup. I don't want you, a young girl, around the jail. Understand?"

"Yes, ma'm. That makes me feel better all over!"

Lauren tucked the blankets around herself. Miranda lit the small window candle and left the room. The fireplace flames dimmed to embers; Lauren was almost sound asleep but awake enough to know the fire could go out momentarily, and too tired to call Miranda to fix it. Lauren heard the clock strike 12 and thought of the witching hour. Her imagination took her back to childhood and a story she heard from her cousin who lived near the coast.

It seems two men decided to walk home late at night after a gathering. The late evening produced no moon in the heavens, or very few stars for guidance. When they neared their residence, they heard something in the tall trees behind the Spanish moss. As they looked up, one man said, "It looks like a big animal up there. Take out your gun and shoot it."

The other said, "I don't have my gun. I left it at home for tonight. But that looks like a big cat."

"Let's get out of here and in the house. The thing is moving. It's too big. Let's get out of here! Run! Let's get out of here. Run!"

The other man was too entranced to move. What was that big cat in the tree? What made it move so suddenly? Cats didn't act that way!

Like the wind that sweeps around the rafters, it came down, attacking the man and pushing him to the ground, taking his money. The incident happened fast and the big animal ran away.

"Help. Help," cried the victim, running to his house. "I've been robbed. I've been robbed."

At that moment his friend came out, toting a shot gun.

"Where is the culprit? That was no cat."

"There he goes. Catch him."

"Stop, you thief," said the man with the gun, running after him. "I'll shoot." The gun went off and the sound echoed throughout into the quiet town. Lauren was told by her cousin that the cat thief still roams the night, watching in the treetops, waiting for victims who never look up.

No wonder, thought Lauren, *why I am scared of the dark.* She eased her mind by thinking about this fear only as a childish notion drummed into her imagination by her cousin's ominous story.

"I must calm myself," she said. "I must think of happier events, like Jim told me to do, and I'll soon be asleep. Ohhhh, where's my fan?"

She felt all around the bed for it, but finally realized she was too tired to continue searching. Lauren fell back on her pillows and closed her eyes. She tossed and turned a bit. In her restlessness, she could not remember if the clock struck one, two or three.

Without provocation, Lauren awoke. A crackling sound that seemed to come from downstairs caused her to sit up abruptly. Miranda screamed. A crash and the sound of breaking glass frightened her.

"Help! Jim! I wish you were here. Help! Miranda. Help!" Lauren shouted.

A rock had shattered her window barely missing a small sperm candle and landing on the floor. Lauren panicked and made her way to the staircase, yelling. "Miranda, Miranda. What happened? Answer me this instant."

The girl stumbled up the stairs in the dark and cried, "Miz Lauren, what should I do?"

"What happened? What happened? Answer me!" screamed Lauren. "Where's the parlor candle? Is it out?"

"Miz Lauren, I didn't light one, but a rock missed me. The broken glass is all over," said the maid in tears.

"Hurry and get a light. Hurry! Get the neighbors. Jim, I wish you were home."

CHAPTER 12

The next day before Lauren awoke, Jim checked over the damage to his house. Miranda stood close by and told him the story of what had happened the night before all over again.

"Miranda, this whole incident has to do with Jeff's case. I suppose some people think him guilty and believe that I should not be on this case at all. Truthfully, I'm afraid this will not be the only time my wife will be frightened. Do as you've been instructed and take care of Lauren. Tell her I'll be home this evening."

"Yes, Massa Jim. I tells her."

Jim mounted his horse and rode to the jail. There he could tell Jeff the whole story of his visit to the Franklin property. The old man was grateful for the work his friend had done for him.

"Jeff, try to think and think hard," said Jim seriously as he gripped the prisoner's shoulders. "Tell me something, anything that will help me in connection with the Turners, Kings and Franklins."

The old man put his hands to his head and closed his eyes.

He moaned. "Da days do go by for me, Marse Benet. Ah knows it ta be afore Christmas, an yes, suh, after Thanksgiving, when I sees Marse King ride pas' me while I was huntin' a rabbit. He coulda been talkin' to Marse George by da way he come ridin'. He rode 'way in a bit o'haste. But Marse George didn't speak to me 'bout matters."

"Jeff, if it just happened to be Sam, what arm was missing? Could you tell?"

"Ah knows, Marse Benet, ah knows it was his lef' arm missin', but suh, it was Capt'n King."

"It's common knowledge James and Sam were the closest of friends," said Jim. "The possibility exists that Sam sent King to George's cabin, but if so, what for?"

Jim surmised that Sam had disappeared from view. Someone might have been protecting him, and Sam might have needed money to escape. Jim suspected Sam could ride for days, even weeks, but it took money to know how to escape for a duration. Turner could not chance being seen anywhere at all. Not being able to borrow money elsewhere, he may have tried his so-called friend, George.

After he left Jeff, Jim thought the next step would be to visit the Turner store and confront Lottie. Under the circumstances, Jim felt this might not be a pleasant experience. He did not want to think about his youth and the way he tried to attract her attention when she visited Scotland. Those days were long ago, and so much time and different events had elapsed.

Lottie was still very pretty, with blond curls and striking blue eyes, petite, a coquette, and charming in her ways of looking and talking with people. Never had Jim met anyone like her before. He knew it was no use thinking about the past, for the future told a more realistic story and relationships changed. Jim wanted to know why relationships had changed. Was it the war? Or the separation from his friends before he came to America? There could be the possibility of the way people change in their attitudes, manners, and habits. Jim wondered if he would find the answer before this case was over. Till tomorrow, Jim thought, as he tipped his hat to an acquaintance on the way to his office.

That evening Jim packed his briefcase and said to Lauren, "I am going to the Turner store as early as possible tomorrow." Lauren looked up at Jim from his desk chair as he spoke. "I know Sam isn't there, but Lottie is. I've got to see her and try to find out if she'll tell me where Sam is." He paused.

"Like any wife, she's going to protect her husband. I'd protect you too, Jim, if anything bad should ever happen," said Lauren.

"I know you would, and I know I'd do the same, but my love, for us there will be no need for that," said Jim. "Sam is somewhere. He's getting by. Something or someone is supporting him and keeping him hidden. There are events in this case I know now I'll never be able to solve."

"Then all the best, my darling, but secretly, I am jealous. Lottie is beautiful. Be careful. In fact, I have not seen her for a long time."

Jim kissed her, pressing on her lips tightly, his arms wrapped around her body securely.

"Jim, I'm breathless now," she said as she fell against his chest.

"See that you stay that way!"

Jim arrived at the store before any customers with their horses or wagons were on the scene. He hoped to chat with Lottie alone. Whenever their paths did cross, Lottie, always in a hurry or busy at some function, dashed away quickly. Jim never told his wife how much he had cared for Lottie, but he continued to convince himself that his silly love affair with her was over. It was easy to understand, Jim thought; her devotion to Sam showed.

Jim quietly opened the door. He saw Lottie working at the counter, probably adding some figures. He turned the "Open" sign to "Closed" to ward off any intruders and watched her in the partial darkness of the entryway. If there appeared any possibility of age on the woman, it was because of Sam and the trying circumstances of their life together. Again, he thought of how the tides of life turned circumstances in another direction, and Jim realized he did not come to the store for love but for the life of an innocent man.

The attorney removed his hat, and at that moment Lottie looked up and smiled. To Jim's surprise, the lady came forward, greeting him as though he were expected. Lottie appeared composed in spite of the strain and frustration Jim convinced himself she could be hiding. She was dressed for work in a plain blue outfit with a small collar. The color complimented her skin and blue eyes.

"Well, sir, have you come for supplies? What brings you here at this hour?"

"Lottie, I'm doing my best to solve the case concerning Jeff David. No doubt you heard he was pronounced guilty. I've hit bottom, although I'm slowly climbing out since certain pieces of evidence came to my attention. These will, of course, help Jeff."

"Why Jim, what has this case got to do with me?"

"With you directly, nothing. I'm doing some checking and hope you will help me."

"People talk about it in the store, but I don't see how I can assist."

"Well, you can. I shouldn't say this, yet I must, for Jeff made no footprints where others insisted he had walked."

"I am not sure just what you mean. I was not at the Franklin home, or at the trial, and only know that Jeff worked for George. He brought the crops to town, but I had no direct dealing with him."

"True, but your husband did. I'd like to see Sam and talk to him. It's very important. Tell me where he is, and I'll answer any questions you have."

"Why Jim, didn't you know? Sam's gone to Greenville. I just received a letter from him. It's here under the counter."

When she retrieved it, Jim examined the letter. It was a love letter and full of incidentals. As Jim studied the letter carefully, Lottie fingered her blond curls, fixing them into shape. When out of patience, she continued adding figures. The letter was dated the day of the murders, December 24, 1877. It was plain that the letter was misleading, for Sam could not have gotten to Greenville on horseback the same day. The trip was over fifty miles, and furthermore, Sam never left home on Christmas in all the years Jim could remember.

"That's very nice, Lottie. Will Sam return soon?"

"You can tell by the letter that it will be awhile. Just as soon as he comes back, I'll tell him you called."

"Sure. Tell him I look forward to seeing him and talking about old times. By the way, what is Sam doing in Greenville?"

"It's business and more business, he says. You know Sam."

Jim knew he did not use his best judgment in relating the fact about the footprints. It would either bring Sam back to defend himself, although he was not accused, or keep him away for a long time. He could not think of any other method to let

Sam know he was onto something. Sam always acted strongly in other situations. Would he be strong enough now to return for questioning? Jim doubted it.

* * * * *

At home that evening, Jim made careful notes of everything which took place at Indigo Springs. Jeff was to be executed in three weeks. In order for Jim to procure a new trial on the after-discovered evidence, he needed to obtain a respite from Governor Wade Hampton in Columbia, so postponement of the execution day could be set beyond the next term of court.

While Jim rode the stage to the city, he gave some thought to Governor Hampton. He liked him, both for his truthfulness and his methods of handling problems in personal life and as governor. Hampton's plans for South Carolina and its progress inspired Jim about this man.

He thought back a few years and recalled hearing about the close election Hampton lost in 1865 from his attorney friend, who came to his home for dinner.

The friend stated, "At the State Democratic Convention, Hampton stood no chance of winning if the black majority remained faithful to the Radicals who supported and fed their needs and wants. By 1876, the methods and vote getting would be dramatic."

"How so?" said Jim.

"In no time at all, sir, someone from Edgefield pressed charges against Hampton, calling him a racist. This charge definitely must be proved wrong. Hampton conducted such a good campaign in proving his honesty and integrity that, when Election Day arrived, he overcame the opposition."

"Sure. I heard that soon afterward, if my memory does not fail me, President Rutherford Hays ordered all the federal troops withdrawn, and the opposition, including the carpetbaggers, faded out of the picture. Hampton was elected, even though there were more votes than voters in some counties," replied Jim.

"Ha, ha. We left that one up to fate," said his friend.

When Jim arrived at the governor's home, his secretary extended cordial greetings to him and put Jim at ease. Then Governor Hampton came out of his office with his hand extended and said, "Jim, good to see you. Come right in. I've heard and read about the David case. I believe you came to see me about it. What can I do for you?"

"I'm honored, Governor," said Jim, shaking Hampton's hand. He noticed that the man had not aged much from when he saw him briefly a few years ago. His hair was only slightly gray. He had a white mustache, somewhat thick eyebrows, kind eyes, and long sideburns.

The men wasted no time and got to the business of law, with Jim explaining all his newly found evidence and requesting a respite.

"I have no problem granting and signing your request, Jim. But how do you think this will help your client?"

"Governor, the first reason is I did not have any of the evidence I related to you at the first trial, since I'd been newly appointed myself. Secondly, if I did not believe Jeff David innocent, I know I would not be here."

"Yes," said the governor, nodding his head. "That much I do understand. Keep me informed. This case looks engaging, and I am interested in its outcome. Now, I will need you to repeat this to Attorney General Conner, so the respite can be granted. Let's go to his office."

Since there were no court stenographers in South Carolina, Jim kept a full set of trial notes, and Judge Mackey did the same. A motion for a new trail would not be possible before a judge who did not preside at the first trial because the state solicitor had to agree on a prepared statement of the written evidence. With written testimony, it enabled the lawyer to draw on clear and concise statements. The judge hearing the motion could evaluate the old and new evidence to see how the guilty verdict came about. Solicitor Cothran insisted the motion be made only before the judge who tried the case. Jim argued with Cothran, but to no avail, for both men knew that in South Carolina's system of rotation, Judge Mackey would not return for three years.

Time again became the essence of importance, since it would be many months before the judge returned. Jim hastened to Columbia and managed to obtain an extended respite for a longer period of time. He also answered questions concerning the case from the governor's private secretary, Major Wade Manning.

After the business of the respite was completed, Jim was ready to leave.

"Say Jim, before you go, the governor would like to see you for a minute or two. Do you mind?" said Major Manning, looking at Jim to see his reaction.

"No," said Jim, looking straight at him. "I don't mind."

"Come on, I'll escort you there," replied the secretary putting his hand on Jim's shoulder. Jim followed him, somewhat perplexed, hoping nothing was wrong.

Hampton saw Jim and said, "It's good to see you. Sit down. Make yourself comfortable. Don't be nervous. I've got some news that might help Jeff's case."

The governor stood beside the attorney and bent over close to Jim's face and spoke. "I know you are anxious to get back, and time may be important to you. I want to say a few words and promise I won't keep you. It's a good idea, I think, to hire a private detective to tail the murderer or murderers. It'll be paid for out of my contingent fund. What do you think?"

Jim hesitated a moment and replied, "On the whole, it sounds like a good idea, but will he be a good enough detective to follow through on the evidence?"

"Yes, but I caution you that no information from your notes should be given to the detective. That way he'll have to find his own evidence," said the governor.

"Let's give it a try. I hope some trail can be found, but I fear it may be too late."

"Good. He'll be to your office in no time at all."

Jim, relieved that the meeting was over, thanked Hampton and went on his way.

CHAPTER 13

Before Jim returned from Columbia with the second respite, the private detective slipped into Jim's office and startled Billy. "Yes, sir. Can I help you?" said the clerk, taken aback by the man's sudden presence.

Billy could tell the stranger wasn't from the area. By the way he stood at the desk, the clerk noticed something city-bred about him. He positioned his body and feet differently than the citizens in town. If he was the detective, Billy thought, he probably solved a couple of bizarre cases. Billy couldn't help but notice him because he was dressed in a mixture of colors. His jacket had brown tones, his shirt was a faded blue. He wore black pants with cowboy boots that looked too big for him. His hair was red, and he had freckles all over is face. He was of medium height and came up to Billy's forehead since the clerk was tall and slim. The stranger appeared about 30-40 years old. His weight gain was apparent around the middle. When he spoke, he used some kind of accent which Billy thought was fake.

"I'm looking for Mr. Benet. Is he here?"

"I'm Billy, Mr. Benet's clerk. You must be the detective the governor told us about."

Somewhat surprised at being recognized, the detective took a step away from the young clerk. "I need Mr. Benet."

"It's for sure he won't be back for a day or two. He went to

Columbia to get a respite for Jeff David. It's the second one, you know."

"Where's the hotel? Someplace I can stay till I can see him. Now, don't breathe a word to anyone that I'm here. I want to have a look around."

"No sir! Not a sound. See, we're the only ones in the office, so nobody knows."

"Good! Where's the hotel?"

"Across the street and up one block," said Billy, fascinated by the presence of a private detective as well as the man's dress. "Mister, I almost forgot! What's your name?"

"Bret Parry," said the man, going out the door.

Billy exclaimed, "Sure is exciting having you! By gosh, if you find the killers, you'll be famous! I wonder if that's your real name. I wonder! Wait till Jim gets back. Won't he be surprised!"

Out on the street, Bret walked toward the hotel. People stared at this new person and his dress. He became annoyed and smart-mouthed a couple of townsfolk he caught looking at him. Fortunately, they did not hear what he said as he walked on to his destination, thinking himself humorous.

In his hotel room, he changed his clothes, disguised his hair under a wig and put on a mustache. This way he could begin work. He planned several disguises and interviews of people in and around Indigo Springs. First he walked to the bench in the square where unknown to him, Judge Mackey had stopped when he came to town. An old farmer with a cane and white beard occupied half of the bench. He looked at Bret. Before he could speak, the detective asked about the murder, using no accent. "Good afternoon, sir. It's a bright day, isn't it? As you can see, I am new in town and heard about these murders. Can you explain? What's the world coming to?"

"It's terrible what's goin' on. Just terrible! I was at the Franklin place the day of the murder. Sister and brother, you know. Hard workin' you bet! I kep' a smellin' this tobaccy. We went into the Franklin house after standin' outside a long time. Yes, sir, I can smell tobaccy anywhere. I kep' a smellin' it."

"Anyone smoking that day? Did you notice?"

"Yes, sir! Patrick O'Dell, the newest Irishman, livin' near the Franklins. It's a sweet tobaccy, and sure as you bet, I kep' a smellin' it."

"I'll be. He sounds suspicious to me!"

Immediately Bret searched for O'Dell's farm and watched him for a couple of days. He noticed O'Dell going in and out of his barn many times and decided to report him. The man grew tobacco, a sweet-smelling brand, and Bret was sure he had his man. He changed his clothes again and appealed to the Solicitor to arrest the Irishman on the basis that the old man kept smelling the odor after the murder. In the process and the course of events, O'Dell was tried and acquitted with considerable speed. Jim was furious at the detective's accusations, and he left the courtroom abruptly and headed home.

He passed some neighbors, but no one looked at him or spoke.

"No doubt people are upset at what happened to O'Dell. Guess they will take it out on me. For the time being, this is better than throwing stones through the window," said Jim, still grumbling to himself at what happened to a good citizen.

The outspoken citizens followed Jim and denounced him

for not solving the case. The tallest and strongest man in the group stepped forward and tried to grab Jim by the arm. Jim was quick and stepped ahead faster to avoid the man's touch. The man asked loudly, "How long is it going to be before there is a conclusion in this case? We know Jeff is guilty. We want justice now."

"You'll get your justice in good time," answered Jim.

"Can't hear you. Speak louder. All of us want to hear you," replied the strong man.

The man followed on Jim's heels. The attorney, not wanting a confrontation with the man or his group, hurried down small streets. Jim approached residences and property he knew the group would not want to be arrested for trampling on. Jim knew he was safe for the moment.

Some people knocked on his door early in the morning and spoke rudely to him for allowing someone like Parry to interfere with the law. "If you don't solve this case soon, we, as citizens of this community, will take the law into our own hands and hang Jeff David," said a short man with a gun belt around his waist. "Do something or we will."

The small crowd that had assembled roared in approval.

Jim snatched his hat and walked through the crowd, not looking at the angry stares. He felt the make-believe knives they had on his back in their anger. When he opened his office door, Billy was waiting for him.

"Billy! The first thing we must do is send Bret on his way before he does more damage than good. He'll anger the town more, and he certainly did Mr. O'Dell and the community. I've got to send him somewhere."

"Send him to Greenville. You can make up some story to

get him out of the way. Those people were sure angry. They passed the window this morning on the way to your house. I could hear them. I also heard that the man who writes the newspaper column is saying Jeff should be hanged soon."

"Inform the sheriff. I don't want that to happen to an innocent man. DuPre will take him to Columbia for awhile till this lynching sentiment calms down. As far as our famous detective is concerned, tell him to be ready to go to Greenville. Take him to the Franklin house and show him the footprints, if they are still there, and make sure he heads to Greenville. God knows what he will find, but that is where the murderers headed."

Time passed without alarming incidents to the David case, and Jeff returned to his old cell in Abbeville. Jim had to travel to Columbia again to obtain a third respite. On the stage coach, he had a worried expression on his face. Jim preferred to say nothing to the passengers, but keep to his own thoughts about Jeff. A woman traveler spoke up.

"Oh, Mr. Benet, did you know Judge Mackey would be in Columbia? He left quickly on an earlier coach. Said he had some important business. Too bad you could not have traveled together. He would be company for you."

"Yes, ma'm," said Jim softly. No one would understand that he was really worried by the woman's statement. Would his hopes for Jeff be dimmed further? What did the judge want in Colombia?

Judge Mackey sat in Governor Hampton's office, his expression intent as he smoked a cigar and sipped on blackberry wine. "Governor, you know as well as I do the black fiend's guilty. He knew the Franklins, their habits, and where the money was. When all quieted on Christmas Eve, that's when the Franklins sat down for their Christmas meal. They ate, and he killed them. Later on, he threw things around and broke everything the in cabin for the money."

"Far as I know of the case, Judge, the Davids had no money."

"True, none was found in their cabin, but don't forget it, they could give to friends to hold, or hide it some place not known to anyone. They had time."

"Judge, it seems as though Jeff's guilt has to be proven. Has he confessed yet?"

"Well, sir, I am glad you asked that. I've got a plan." The judge took a big sip of wine. "We'll place David on the scaffold in court. He'll confess. I guarantee it!"

"Judge, that sounds bizarre!"

"Governor, I guarantee it!"

* * * * *

After Judge Mackey left the governor's office, the attorney general signed the respite that Jim waited for. Quietly, the attorney general spoke into the lawyer's ear, "Jim, the governor has made a request to see you. Guess it won't take long, but you can go to his office now."

Jim hurried down the hall and was quickly led to Governor Hampton who waited for him.

"Good to see you, Jim. Come in. Sit down. I have something to tell you. I am limited because of my schedule, so I will be brief. First of all, Judge Mackey was here earlier, and you can be sure he spoke his piece."

"I can imagine, Governor. No, I did not know he was here. What did he want?"

"It's this way, Jim. The judge believes David is guilty. Mackey wants him hung in court."

"Governor! That's the worst punishment I have ever heard of. Don't do it! No one has heard the evidence. I don't want Jeff to die beforehand even from a heart attack."

Jim got up from his chair and went to the window. He put his head in his hands and could have cried for the old man.

Hampton put his hand on Jim's shoulder. "Take heart and be of good courage. Jim, the judge is not the only one with a plan. I agree with you, but don't tell Mackey. After I granted the judge's wishes, I too thought the idea gruesome. I don't want this act of torture completed."

"How in heavens name will it not be carried out?"

"Here's what you'll do. Take this third respite, but keep it the deepest of secrets. We'll grant the judge his request, but you step in before the rope is pulled. This event is not to be carried out to the fullest. I'll give you other necessary papers."

"Thank heaven, governor. This act will be hard enough as it is, but I will do as you say."

"Bless you, Jim."

* * * * *

Days later Jim read the news of the governor's decision to hang Jeff in court in the Abbeville paper. He let the newspaper slump in his lap and sat straight up at his desk.

"So, he granted Judge Mackey's request after all," said Jim softly. "I know I will need to see Jeff now. I hoped this ordeal would pass, but it did not. It would be hard and strenuous for

Jeff, but the secret held tightly in my vest pocket gives me strength to go on."

Jim didn't know exactly what he would say to the prisoner. Words could not come easy at a time like this. *I am not dying,* Jim thought, *but how do I tell someone else he is going to die, but yet, he is not going to die!* Even Billy did not question his boss as he left the office. Jim passed the courthouse and heard the pounding. Several onlookers were curiously watching the proceedings from the courthouse door. Some were astonished at what they saw happening.

"By gosh, looks like they're gonna build a scaffold right at the court," said a middle-aged man wearing thick glasses. "Never saw it like that before."

"Don't ya know," said a bald headed man, "they want that David man to confess. Judge Mackey is tellin' 'um at the drugstore now."

Jim wanted to shout that Jeff was not guilty, but he knew it would be of no use now and might only lead to trouble of another sort. Anyway, Jeff's unwarranted sentence had been bestowed upon him by the adverse tendencies of others whose perspectives on life and its course should be pronounced by them to be best decision before any further evidence was produced remained repulsive to Jim.

As Jim was led into Jeff's cell, Jeff saw him right away. The prisoner cried, "Marse Jim, don' le' me all alone with this burden put upon me! If you be da one to be wif me, ah'll make it ta heaven."

Jim sat beside Jeff on the cot. The old man was in pain mentally and physically, but Jim could arouse no suspicion whatsoever. He refused Jeff as kindly as he could. He hugged him and said, "Jeff, be strong in the Lord. Remember, the good Lord will support you all the day long. He will never leave you, never."

"Marse Jim, I scared. Scared. What'll I do? What'll I do?"

Jim felt himself weakening. Jeff held his hand tightly. His eyes pleaded for Jim to stay, comfort him and give him encouragement.

"Ah don't know what to do, Marse Jim. What'll become wif my family?"

Jim couldn't wait a minute longer. His stomach did turns and he felt as if he were going to vomit. He jumped up and called the jailer to release the door latch.

"Marse Jim, Marse Jim, don' leave me. Don' leave me. Ah beg of you. Will da good Lord know ah didn' do it? Marse Jim, Marse Jim!"

"Yes, yes," shouted Jim as he swiftly left the cell.

"Pray wif me, Marse Jim. Pray wif me!"

"Yes, yes," was the faint reply.

Jim put the important respite in his office safe hidden in a closet. He had no doubts about anyone knowing what would happen to Jeff in less than a few days' time. Jim read where the Abbeville newspaper reported they could say that no respite was given. Nevertheless, Jim remained confident that he himself, Governor Hampton and his private secretary officially knew the situation.

On Friday morning early before the sun came up, Jim had Billy contact Sheriff DuPre, who came directly over to Jim's office. Behind closed doors, with only one small candle lit, Jim explained Judge Mackey's decision to have Jeff hanged that day.

"This is unheard of, Jim. It's grotesque! I find this difficult to comprehend. In all, I will co-operate with you and definitely watch for the last moments. I suggest the doctor from Due West be there. He is usually the attending physician at executions in case the victim has a heart attack when the rope and black kerchief go around his head."

"I don't have any quarrel with that," said Jim. "The doctor is not to know anything though."

"It's agreed. I want to mention," said the sheriff, "that Jeff is asking for you. You can come any time before the event. He's having a hard, hard time accepting it all."

"Sheriff, I could not come. I can barely stand it. I am nervous. If anything goes wrong, I will never forgive myself. I don't know what to do."

"Jim, I will perform all the movements slow and deliberate. I think you can tell the moment when the cord will be pulled if you stand very close to the stage. You can be sure I'll watch you too."

"There's one more item, in case you haven't looked at the setting. It's a small barn-like enclosure outside the courthouse. Jeff will have a preacher present. The public can see it all if they wish. The courtroom is not big enough to hold a scaffold as the judge wanted," said DuPre leaving Jim's office. "See you soon, Jim."

* * * * *

At the appointed time, Jim made sure that he carried the respite securely in his pocket, ready to pull put at the appropriate moment. He was visibly nervous as he left the office. Even

Billy bowed his head in a moment of silence. Jim watched an entourage of people surround Jeff as they approached the structure. When Jim came closer to the scaffold, he saw Jeff climb the stairs and turn around. Jim wanted to shout, "Jeff, I am here," but he knew it would be of little comfort.

Jim stood within earshot of the scaffold, as close as he would get to a hanging. Sheriff DuPre inconspicuously acknowledged the attorney's presence. Jeff started to cry as the black preacher read verses from the Bible and prayed. The witnesses, the doctor, the deputies and the curious listened in silence. Some bystanders prayed and others closed their eyes.

With assistance, Jeff mounted the scaffold step. His ankles and hands were tied. The small audience sighed as the noose was put around his neck. Tears flowed down Jeff's cheeks. He cried out in spite of his pain. "Massa George and Miz Drusilla, ah is comin' with you to Jesus. You knows I did not kill you. Ah am goin' to die right now."

Jeff stood erect like the part Indian he was and looked up to heaven.

The sheriff read the sentence of the court. Jim felt for the respite in his pocket. The black cap was put over Jeff's head. Next, the noose around Jeff's neck was made tighter.

"Oh, God," cried Jim. "Stop! Stop! Jeff will not be hanged. I have a respite in my hand signed by Governor Hampton. Here it is."

DuPre read the respite and ordered Jeff released of his ordeal and sent back to prison.

The spectators were amazed and astonished. One man whispered to another, "Maybe this was acted out. A hanging is a hanging. I never experienced something like this before."

The doctor from Due West reported that Jeff's pulse went down low when the black cap was put over his head. At its removal the former servant's pulse quickened. He knew nothing of the respite. No one, thought Jim, can control his pulse.

Jim strolled breathlessly back to his office. He prayed God would forgive him for putting a human being through a torture for a confession that never came. "What an ordeal. Jeff must be exhausted and drained of all feeling. If, Lord, I did wrong in letting this happen, I know I have paid the penalty this day."

CHAPTER 14

The days and the months passed. Governor Hampton got elected to the U.S. Senate. Jim rejoiced for the governor because he believed Hampton deserved to win this nomination and election.

Jim put down the paper with the governor's story on his office desk and closed his eyes and concentrated. Then he called to Billy in the other room and said, "What do you know about the new man in office? You know, the new governor. What does he think and feel? How will he help my case?" Jim tossed his hands in the air. "What does he even know about Jeff David? How am I going to convince this new man in the governor's chair of Jeff's innocence?"

"Wow!" Billy answered. "Mr. Benet, you sure ask a lot of questions I don't have the answers to." Billy got up from his chair and straightened his tie. He grabbed his notebook and hustled into Jim's office.

"Billy, Governor Hampton was forthright and honest and stood by his word. I am apprehensive about this other man."

Billy stood with the pencil between his teeth and just looked at Jim, saying nothing.

"The governor was not afraid to be alone in his thinking and ended up to be right about any outcome most of the time. In any form, there can be no procrastination. I must have the answers when I see the new man."

"Sure, sure, Jim, I mean, Mr. Benet," said Billy still not knowing what to say.

Jim pounded his desk with his fists once and Billy dropped his pencil.

He said, "Billy, I've made up my mind to face this new situation. Come over here. You're going to have to help me face this new governor!"

"Mr. Benet, how?"

Billy stood near Jim and held his pencil and paper, ready to write. He had never seen Jim so serious and pensive.

"Look, Billy, I just want to get a reaction from you on what I will say to the new governor—providing he gives me a chance. It's just for practice. That's all. Don't look so scared!"

"Gosh, Mr. Benet, I think you should just be yourself," said Billy, flipping his suspenders. "I don't know much about this new man. I haven't heard much gossip around town either. It sure is a problem. Wait a minute! I got it. Just keep repeating and keep repeating that Jeff is not guilty. How's that?"

"Well, Billy, that's a start. I want to leave tomorrow morning as soon as the stage comes in. So, let me do some rehearsing on you. Now, how will this message sound?"

* * * * *

While packing his necessary papers at home early in the morning, Jim threw them in the case he would carry on the journey. Lauren stood by and watched him grab them in small stacks and drop them in a bag. Jim seemed to be taking everything. He dropped some papers, paying no attention to his own movements. Lauren picked them up. She set them on Jim's desk. He looked up and saw her staring him.

"Honestly, Lauren, I am shaken. This Governor Simpson may view Jeff's case differently. I…I had a premonition this would happen to me. When we had that meeting at Sam's house a long time ago, things did not work out."

"Premonitions are not always true. Jim, you think too hard on the subject and turn the situation into something you feel you can't master."

"I had these thoughts at the office. I wanted to get this out of my mind, but it stayed there. I imagined what Simpson would be like…and…."

"There you go. You imagined! Your imagination ran away from you and you felt differently. Now think clearly. Maybe this man is not an ogre after all!"

"Yes, I do try to think clearly and put the pieces together, and this new governor does not fit the pieces. He views situations differently, which I can understand. I'm used to disagreement, but his reasoning on certain events in politics is far to the other side from mine. I've given so much to this case that if it fails, I may fail with it."

Jim fell into his chair. "Lauren, have I taken care of all I need for the meeting? Yes, I guess I have. I'll need every paper and word that's written on it."

Lauren put her arms around him and said, "Jim, you can't fail. You won't fail. With your knowledge and know-how of this case and all the evidence you've discovered, you'll be able to convince the governor that Jeff's respite is needed. You have what it takes; you have taken everything."

"Maybe I have taken everything. I know I don't want to

talk about Judge Mackey."

"No, don't, unless you have to."

Jim glanced out the window and could see the stage pull into its stop across the street. He knew he would have to leave in a few minutes. He took out his handkerchief and wiped his brow. He pulled Lauren on his lap and pressed his cheek to hers. She was receptive and held him tightly.

He placed his finger under her chin and raised her chin to his touching her heart-shaped lips. He kissed her, but not passionately, for he was too nervous. The kiss seemed warm and tender-hearted. As their lips touched, they pressed firmly upon each other with a love and trust they sensed was unique to them. Jim knew he would need her when he returned.

* * * * *

When Jim entered Governor Simpson's office, the governor motioned with his hand to come forward and sit down. He looked intently at a report he held in his hands and did not look up at Jim for a few minutes. Jim glanced around the office. Pictures and memorabilia had changed. Governor Simpson's idea of decorating was the plainer the better. Simpson finally looked up at Jim with a wrinkled forehead and studied him with care. He did not greet him, but was brusque and irritable in his manner and voice. He said to his visitor, "You have four weeks until January 15 to show me Jeff David is innocent. I am not convinced of Jeff's innocence, so there must be further proof presented to me. Can you do this?"

Annoyed at the governor's abrupt and closed-minded approach to the case, Jim could not help but reply, "Sir, you know it is an impossibility for me to provide you with further proof before that time, but my pledge to you is that he will not be hanged."

"Then when can you do so? The sooner the better."

"I brought many papers with me. Some can be left here for your reading and sent back to me at your convenience."

The governor asked a few more questions concerning the case, but both men parted without a handshake or cordial farewell. Jim went into the hallway of the office and closed the door. He exclaimed as he looked down, "What will I do?"

"Jim, Jim, remember me," said a voice Jim recognized but could not place. He examined the room and saw Secretary Manning rushing up to him. Jim, relieved at who he saw, smiled and shook hands with the secretary.

"I wanted to talk to you before you left. It's important."

"I hope you've got some good news to convey to me," said Jim. "I just saw the governor. Our meeting was not cordial at all. You know, I am still working to free Jeff David. I am distressed at what may happen next," he exclaimed, feeling worried.

"Jim, let's get over to this corner where it is quieter. I don't like telling you this, but you've got another battle ahead to free Jeff and prove he's innocent. I heard the governor's sister-in-law from Atlanta tell other prominent people on several occasions that she was sure Jeff was of bad character and guilty."

"Now, why would she say things like that?"

"Because Jeff, who was sold to the Franklins, belonged to the governor's sister-in-law's father. He sold Jeff to George Franklin."

"But that's nothing against Jeff."

"I know, but you're up against what everybody else says.

My idea would be to write Senator Hampton about your situation. He was sympathetic before, and, before I forget, it better be mentioned that Judge Mackey talks of Jeff David's guilt around the state in his travels. It's bad policy. You know how some people are."

"I appreciate your news and concern. Thanks, friend. I'll head across the hall to the library and write Senator Hampton immediately."

*   *   *   *   *

Senator Hampton did intercede as soon as he could. Prior to Christmas, he went directly to Governor Simpson's office to talk with him about the David case.

After the senator and the governor greeted each other, Hampton pulled his chair right up to the desk where the Governor sat and said, "What is this I hear of your not supporting the attorney, Jim Benet, and his client, Jeff David? Jeff is innocent—innocent of any crime. Read the new evidence again, and you'll see I am right. Don't throw this case to the hounds. Jeff is innocent and Jim knows it. He can prove it. Give him a chance to show Jeff's innocence."

"I am not sure, Wade. He lived right on the property, and I'm considering the fact that he did it, since many like him want their way."

"Now, you have not thoroughly read the new evidence. Remember two tracks were found. They headed toward Greenville. There were two men, not one. One of them was not Jeff. Jeff is not strong enough to do this terrible deed. He's too passive. One of your relatives said this. You know it. Besides they said at the jail, he often has stomach pains and can't eat except what his wife cooks. That doesn't sound like a murderer to me."

"I hope you're right, Wade, since you have worked on this before. I will concede this time, but, well, we'll see. I will grant the respite. Office boy, office boy! I want this sent to Mr. James Benet, attorney in Abbeville right away."

"Thanks, friend. You'll be glad you did. Now, let's have lunch sent in."

* * * * *

Jim received the respite for a new trial. He made plans for it to take place in November, 1880, where Judge Mackey would preside. It was nearly three years after Jeff's conviction. When the judge opened court again, Jim was fully prepared to handle any events that might happen during the trial. The pressure of public opinion was against him more than ever.

He still believed he had the situation well in hand and that no one was aware of the evidence presented in the affidavits. He told Judge Mackey, "I make a motion for a new trial." He looked up at the judge who seemed to be impressed. Jim went ahead and read the papers slowly. He enunciated carefully. He emphasized the words and phrases relating how the past statements flatly contradicted the testimony under which Jeff was convicted.

Judge Mackey listened attentively, but somehow Jim did not trust him. He kept in mind what Secretary Manning told him the judge had said about Jeff in his travels around the state.

The state solicitor stood up and sneered at Jim. He said, "Your honor, a new trial would be of no use. The first trial was fair in every way. A new trail would take too much time. It would be a waste of time for all concerned. I recommend we refuse the motion."

Mackey sat back in his bench and looked at the two lawyers. He pretended to be concentrating for a moment. Then he cleared his throat and said, "We have all heard the motion presented for a new trial on the after-discovered evidence. The affidavits presented by the distinguished counsel meet the requirements of the rules of evidence. The evidence presented is clearly after-discovered and could not have been established at the trial three years ago."

Jim's body tingled with excitement. He felt the warmth of confidence and the steadiness of security. In no time at all, however, he became apprehensive since all eyes were on Judge Mackey. Jim broke out in a cold sweat. The perspiration ran down his forehead. He reached in his pocket for a handkerchief and, as inconspicuously as possible, began wiping the cold droplets off his brow and neck. *If prayers can be answered, Lord, tell me, what is Mackey up to? I wish I could read his mind. I thought of everything I could think of for Jeff. Oh, the judge is talking again. He is taking more time than usual.*

The judge shifted in his chair, trying to be more comfortable. He regrouped his papers, folding some and putting others in a pile. He looked at the people in court. He realized he had their full attention. He sat back in his chair and appeared confident.

"Earlier counsel had not the time nor the opportunity to obtain evidence which has now been submitted," said Judge Mackey. "The counsel has proved himself in a befitting manner without fee or reward or the hope of it. The court is deeply impressed and does have little doubt, that if the counsel had presented the evidence at the trial, possibly the verdict may have been different, and if true, may have been a verdict of not guilty."

Mackey paused for a few seconds as if pleased with his pronouncement. He had more to say, so he cleared his throat again and continued. "Three years have gone by and, with regret, the court deems it necessary that it does not now have the power to order a new trial, so solicitor, sir, kindly prepare the motion refusing a new trial."

The solicitor smiled and nodded at the judge and said, "I'll be glad to do it."

Jim was flabbergasted! He began to hurt inside. He felt the pain in his heart go up to his throat. He turned from the judge and the solicitor. He saw the faces in court smiling and satisfied. No, he cried to himself, you will not win. He turned again and started to rush over to Judge Mackey. He jumped across Jeff and the table, landing on the floor. Mackey looked at Jim surprised, as if wondering what he wanted coming so fast toward him. A few steps away from the judge, Jim reminded himself to control his anger and stopped short of the bench where Mackey sat. Jim thought for a moment. He regained his composure and spoke firmly.

"Your Honor, allow me to prepare the order to represent the grounds for your refusal. I am asking this in order to appeal to the Supreme Court."

The judge smiled and said, "Your request is granted. I'll sign the order."

The lawyer gave notice of appeal. After this notice was completed, it was again necessary to obtain a respite. Jim felt better about the outcome now since he knew that Simpson had been made Chief Justice and an interim governor was in place.

On the appointed day in Columbia, Jim presented the appeal to the court and almost immediately one of the judges said, "There is an error committed here in the documentation. I can see it in the written appeal. It's an error by Judge Mackey, stating that he had no power to grant a new trial because the first one was long ago. Mr. Benet, your case is upheld, and it will be ordered back to the Circuit Court."

A new judge read Mackey's order of refusal and the Supreme Courts Court's reversal and granted a new trial. Jim obtained another respite and prepared once more for Jeff's court session for November, 1881.

Prior to the trial, Jim met the county supervisor, Mr. Edwards. They talked quietly, not wanting anyone to hear them.

"Now repeat for me exactly what you want me to do at the Franklins," said Mr. Edwards.

"I want you to draw a chart showing the woods, stumps, persimmon bushes, paths, fences, pig-pen, the old cabin where the Franklins lived, and the sandbank and Jeff's cabin. It must be accurate. I cannot stress that enough. Public sentiment is much higher and against Jeff."

"I'll do it, Jim. I like your persistence in getting the old man freed, especially if he did not commit the murder."

"Good. I'll pick your chart up in a few days."

Jim left the supervisor's office and walked up the stairs to the first floor. "Good morning," Jim said to a lawyer acquaintance who passed him. But the man walked away and did not answer Jim. The same thing happened as he passed a second attorney. Jim knew the feeling ran high that Jeff should be hanged. No one in the town spoke to him or Lauren. *This is sad,* thought Jim, *but I'll feel sorry for the community if an innocent man is hung.* He returned to his office where Billy shouted, "Good morning, Mr. Benet. How shall we start the day?"

The only good news Benet received after a while were the list of 36 petit jurors whose names were published in the county paper. This was encouraging, since Jim was elated to have at least 20 to choose from who were considered intelligent men. By the power of Jeff's right to object, Jim felt sure that a fair jury could be selected.

"Billy, I may have more for you to do soon, but it is imperative I see Bob Nickels. Don't tell anyone. I've an idea regarding the persimmon saplings, so I'll be at his place for a time. Tell Lauren I'll be late."

"Sure thing, Mr. Benet. Bet you got a few surprises goin'."

As soon as Jim arrived at Bob's, he was greeted warmly. "Jim this is an honor," said Bob. "Sit in this comfortable chair. I heard about how the town is treating you from Mr. Watkins. I want you to know it is not the same here. Glad you came. What can I do for you?"

Bob's wife served coffee and homemade bread, which Jim devoured with relish. He got to the business at hand when the last bite was swallowed.

"Bob, I want you to help me with the persimmon saplings. It seems Gideon thinks he is an expert. I want to prove him wrong. I think there's a way we can do this. Let's talk about it."

* * * * *

When the time came for the court session, Judge Frasier presided. He was a quiet man who listened more than he talked. You could be standing next to him at a gathering, and he barely said a word, thought Jim. Frasier had little hair, slightly pink cheeks, and was short, but not overweight. Jim felt fortunate in his selection of the jury, which included business men, planters, and farmers.

The Nestor of the Bar tapped Jim and said, "I feel like old Jeff, not guilty in selecting such a jury."

After the jury retired to elect a foreman, the trial proceeded with James King, Judah Arnold, and Gideon O'Neil.

King no longer had the confident responses he had at the first trial. He admitted in a softer voice, "Jeff David did tell me about the money in the brown fur trunk found in Drusilla's room. In answer to your question, Mr. Benet, I did…I did forget all about it at the first trial."

"What about the footprints you claim were Jeff's? Tell the court about that incident, Mr. King."

James bowed his head. He could barely be heard and said, "Some men who I never saw before assisted me in pulling Jeff over to one side. We made him walk and leave footprints in the area we thought we'd use as evidence against him. After that, we took him further off to the side, and one of the men I had never seen before tied a rope around his neck. Jeff admitted his guilt when we hung him and he nearly strangled."

"That's all. You may step down," said Jim.

There was not a sound in the courtroom as King testified. He received scornful and disrespectful looks from the people as he passed the benches. He whispered a soft "Thank you" as he passed Jim. He was grateful for being let off easy.

Judah Arnold was the next witness called. He did not appear like the same man. His black beard was shaved off, and he seemed reluctant to look at anyone since he lost his identi-fying trademark. When Jim questioned him about Jeff's foot-prints, he answered, "Ah'm not positive the footprints were Jeff's. A lot of people jus' milled around all over the place. Ah mean, I guess the footprints were not Jeff's."

There were a few more important questions by Jim, who wanted to clear things up, but it was obvious that Judah no longer supported King.

Gideon O'Neil came forward immediately when his name was called. He took the stand in a new brown suit. He straight-ened his tie and took the oath on the Bible. He made himself comfortable in the chair on the witness stand and smiled at a few acquaintances huddled on the benches. He waited for Jim to question him.

Jim approached the witness stand cautiously. He knew O'Neil's declaration about the persimmon bushes, but he care-fully wanted to contradict the defendant.

"Mr. O'Neil, we are all acquainted with you in this court-room and know you to be a man of good character. You must be aware that the testimony you give could put Jeff to death. Gideon O'Neil, do you solemnly swear and wholeheartedly believe you could not be mistaken about the stain on George's knife blade?"

"Mr. Jim, I knew I'd be closely questioned on this, so I made several experiments taking samples of cut saplings and checking the stain on the knife. I can recognize the stain at any time. There's none like it. It's yellowish."

"Yes," said some voices. The judge called for order. The courtroom fell silent. The disorder of the first trial had disap-peared. Jim handed Gideon a pasteboard box that unknown to everyone else, contained 12 newly-purchased knives of the same size and make as George's. Each numbered knife was used by Billy a few days earlier at Jim's instruction. Billy cut a sample from the saplings of twelve different trees. A record was kept to identify them. Only one knife cut the persimmon sapling.

"Gideon, I want you to tell the court which knife has the persimmon stain on it," said Jim. Gideon looked at the box. His hands shook as he opened it. It was not heavy. The top came off easy. He seemed amazed at all the knives he saw and the many different stains. At once he began to examine each knife. Gideon looked at the judge and the people in the court-room.

"You know…I jus' know the persimmon stain," Gideon muttered.

"Take your time, Gideon," said Jim, relaxing a bit. "No one wants to rush you, for you stated you could positively identify the stain of the persimmon bush. Tell the jury what stains you do recognize and the number of file marks you see on the back of each blade."

"Ah need to really look at this vera carefully. May I take this to the window for more light?"

"I think the court will not object," said Jim.

O'Neil examined the knives, looking carefully at each one. He examined them again. The court's silence was beyond anything Jim had ever experienced before. He sensed the tension, for not a sigh by anyone expressed itself. After a time, Gideon picked up a knife marked number six. Jim watched him as though the man was going to run away.

"If that's the knife you choose, do you swear that the stain on number six is persimmon?" asked Jim.

Gideon studied the knife, holding it closer to his eyes. He hesitated a moment, and then put it back in the box. "No, it's not like the persimmon stain," he said shaking his head.

Jim came up to the bench and called, "Billy Shill. Come forward with the sealed evidence and hand the sealed paper to the judge to be read as evidence."

The judge opened the sealed paper. He read the message to the court, which said, "The stain on the numbered knife with the persimmon stain is number six."

Jim couldn't hide his emotions. He smiled and shook hands with Billy. He looked at the crowded courtroom of surprised people. They were astonished and began conversing with their neighbors. It was like a bolt of lightning to them, a piece of news they never expected.

Gideon, too, was struck with his own unexpected moment. He was dismissed from the witness box and slipped out passed the crowd of people still chattering about the stain.

Jim almost hugged Jeff, who smiled even though he had stomach pains again. Jeff whispered to Jim, "Ah believe the good Lord is helpin' us, Marse Jim."

During the rest of the trial, the only new evidence introduced was Jeff's shirt with blood stains on the back, none on the front. The volunteer attorney put Jeff on the stand.

Jeff said, "Yes, sir, on the mornin' of December 24, ah killed a hog an' carried the carcass on my back. Yes, sir, I did."

Jim was furious at this attorney. He perceived the shirt to be improper evidence. He felt like choking the upstart who pretended he knew the law.

Bob Nickels took the stand and testified, "The couple, George and Drusilla, never used store bought-candles. I also know for a fact neither did Jeff or his family. The murderers threw everything around, looking for the money. Then something scared them, and as they escaped, they threw the club and candles away. They even bumped into the pens. It should be noted that King and Arnold or any other person could not have found Jeff's tracks where the men swore they did."

Then Billy explained his part with the knives and saplings and swore, "Your honor, I solemnly swear that I did everything correctly regarding the knives and stain. I recorded the stain and numbers accurately and honestly."

"On knife number six," said Jim, "Mr. O'Neil stated it was not persimmon stain. You must reply to the court on that issue."

Jim did not want to leave any doubt about anything, and Billy answered. "Mr. O'Neil is entitled to his opinion, but I know the knife number six to be the persimmon stain. The knife has never cut anything but persimmon, for all 12 knives were just purchased and kept entirely in my possession. Mr. Benet knew this too but did not touch them, or know the numbers I used, or which knife cut the sapling."

The jury nodded at each other in agreement. The young attorney presented a few futile arguments, but Jim interceded with quotes of the law. He disliked this so-called lawyer even more. He approached the jury and showed them that the evidence on which Jeff was convicted previously had been contradicted, like the example of the footprints. This meant the main witness for the State had been discredited.

The murder theory, made clear to them, was presented in question form. Jim asked, "Was there any person at the time near the Franklin area who just might have urgent cause to flee the state? Did he commit a homicide already? Did he need money? Was this a one-armed man? Did he cut the persimmon club? Did he hire or persuade a black man to assist him to rob the old couple of money he knew to be there?"

Jim hesitated a moment and let the men in the box think about the questions he had just asked them. In the meantime, he readied himself for his next comments. "Visualize two robbers at a tall tree, hitching a horse and then stealthily sneaking up to the cabin from behind. The black man checks the back window. He sees George and Miss Drusilla eating supper. George's back is facing the front door, and his sister is facing him at the small table. The burglar knows that all it takes is one blow, but it need not be fatal. Yet the white man must have the money. He could not take the chance and be recognized. So, the companion must spring into the room and stun the couple."

The court listened in silence. Gone were the echoes of the "no" sounds from the first trial. Jim continued. "The blow made the Franklins unconscious and lying on the floor. Then the leader lights the two sperm candles, and each of them rampaged the cabin, searching for the money. The noise does not disturb the old couple at that moment being robbed of their savings.

"The two men find the rolls of bills and search on for more. They find a trunk or two but where are the keys? They pick George's pockets and open the trunk. Then they canvass Miss Drusilla's room and find more money hidden in various places. This drives them on, looking, and searching. The candle gives them the light. They discover the old fur-covered chest under the bed.

"At that moment they hear a sound. When they look up, there stands poor, poor Drusilla, recovered from unconsciousness. She sees the men and knows the robber. She calls him by name! At that instant, the robbery turns into an ugly double murder. The murderers hastily depart."

Jim could sense the jury adapting to his thoughts and convictions. Were they waiting for him to name the murderer? Did anyone on the jury try to guess the murderer? He continued with his address to the jury. "Gentlemen, the one who has just killed Miss Drusilla has the blood-stained club in his hand. As the men escape, they throw the club and sperm candles away. They speedily head for the horse tethered to the pine tree."

The trial continued for four more hours, and in that time Jim noticed that Frank slipped into the courtroom. Jim was pleased but concentrated on making sure that his facts and all the evidence were presented in clear terms to the jury.

Jim called Frank and Bob to the stand to show the jury that the murder had been committed by two men, one white and one black. He wanted the jury to understand Jeff had no connection with the men and set up his designed plan and map of the Franklin locale.

"With the court's permission, let me demonstrate with proof that the double set of prints coming and going between pine trees and the house were not Jeff's."

Jim explained the details and believed he convinced everyone that King and Arnold were not telling the truth earlier. Jim presented the bloody persimmon club and the candles as proof they were hastily discarded by the murderers as they ran and knocked over the pigpens.

"Two men crossed the plowed field as fast as they could.

I'd like the jury to take note of the accurate drawing presented here of the size of the footprints. Remember, one rode the horse, the other walked. I'll need to have testimony of Frank Fuller concerning the club that was cut by a one-armed man."

Frank gave his testimony understandably and clearly proving his statements correct. Jim was relieved and confident. He spoke in a whisper, thanking Frank who passed to take his seat. It was quiet for a moment in the court. Jim knew his next step but wanted to hold back a moment and relax. Judge Frasier had closed his eyes. Jim was glad for the silence and the chance to think of what would come next. Then someone on the court bench stood up. Everyone looked at the one-armed Confederate veteran dressed in uniform. Jim looked at the man in astonishment. The judge opened his eyes, wondering who caused a stir. The veteran spoke.

"Mr. Benet, you have truly proven Jeff not guilty and probably convicted a one-armed man, a man of low esteem."

"Yes, yes," the crowd shouted loudly.

Judge Frasier sounded his gavel as loudly as he could. He shouted, "Order! Order!"

The court became silent. Jim nodded in approval and continued with an account about the wounds of the victims, the pool of blood in which Drusilla's head had lain, and all the drops of blood leading from the table to the bedroom.

Jim called Bob to the witness stand once more to confirm the two sets of tracks in the field, the black man's footprints at the back window, the horse's hoof prints at the pine tree, the club, and the candles.

In the closing statements for the prosecution by the Solicitor, the statements were weakened by the State's witness Dr.

Waddell, the new evidence presented, and the volunteer attorney who tried to interfere whenever he could.

The trial lasted for three days, and at 11:30 a.m. of the third day, Judge Frasier charged the jury to reach a verdict. At midnight they retired into a cold jury room, covering themselves with blankets because there was no fireplace or stove.

"Sheriff DuPre," said the judge, as the sheriff ended a conversation with Frank. "You know to call me first thing when a decision is reached by the jury. Then call the counsel."

"I know. You'll be the first to hear. Your honor, it's late. There won't be much sleep tonight for anyone," and he walked away to talk to the foreman of the jury.

People dispersed, wrapping scarves around their heads, and tied shawls tighter as they came out of court and felt the night air. Outside Bob and Frank complimented Jim for his work on the case. The volunteer attorney casually walked down the courthouse steps, aloof to anyone around him. Jim spotted him. Before anyone could say another word, Jim leaped before him. He swung his hand to pop the young man in the jaw.

"I'm going to get you, you imbecile," said Jim.

"Wait, Jim," said Frank, grabbing Jim's arm.

"Don't do anything you'll be sorry for," shouted Bob, holding Jim's other arm.

The young man, stunned and unaware of any unwarranted action he committed, saw Jim roll up his sleeves. Before anyone could grab Jim again, he took a swing at the attorney and missed, causing the man to fall down the steps.

Jim shouted, "You fool. You could put an innocent man to death by your constant interference."

The young man got up. He was shaken but unscathed and

looked at Jim in amazement as if to say "what did I do?"

"Come on, Jim, let us take you home," said Bob hanging onto Jim's arm.

Frank replied, "Yes, I've got my carriage over here. Let's go, Jim."

Order was restrained outside the court. Since most of the crowd hurriedly left in the cold night, few saw what happened."

CHAPTER 15

Jim opened the door of his home. Before entering, he looked up and down the street. It was dark and quiet and full of solitude. A feeling of exhaustion overwhelmed his body. After three days of trial, he wanted to rest for a few minutes, sit down, and enjoy the peace. He pushed the door open farther; the hallway presented a deep, blue. A glitter from the fireplace guided his way to a comfortable chair. He sunk down in its cushions. Lauren must have gone to bed hours ago because the trial lasted so long.

Jim put his head back. He took pride in all that he accomplished to arrive at this point in the trial. He knew that he prayed with all his might that Jeff would be free at last.

To himself he said, "I am certain, Lord, that You led me on this quest and gave me the courage to face any adversity. Let me thank You for Your guidance and for Your love of this poor sinner. The decision rests in Your hands, but I fear nothing anymore or no one. I am sure the jury will come to the right decision. It's in Your hands."

Jim fell into a light sleep. A burnt log rolled over in the fireplace. The embers gave off just enough heat to keep the room warm and cozy. When the clock struck one, Jim woke up startled, but found a glass of grog on the table left there for him. Lauren must have placed it there when she went to bed. He took a sip and no sooner had the glass touched his lips when he heard a loud knock. The deputy said loudly, "We've got a verdict. The sheriff went to the hotel to get the judge, and the solicitor is being sent for."

Jim grabbed his hat, gloves, and a small briefcase, which had fallen to the floor.

"Here I am," said Jim to the deputy as he opened the door. "This case was a four-year struggle, and soon we will know the answer!"

The courtroom was still cold and three small hand lamps were burning. Several worn and tired people congregated close to the light. It looked as though they did not go home. Some huddled together and watched the movements of Jim, Judge Frasier, and the sheriff who brought in a sleepy Jeff David.

The judge sat on his bench and yawned. He concentrated on getting his composure for the verdict and finally got into a comfortable position in his chair.

Jeff sat pensively. He clutched his hands as his knees began to shake. He looked at Jim, who gave him a nod of assurance. Jim tried to contemplate the look on the jury's faces and saw in the dim light that their faces were grim. He said softly to Jeff, "I hope they only look that way because they are tired."

The judge conducted a short formality, and the deputy clerk unfolded the record. He turned the paper around, but it appeared as though he could not see it. The sheriff handed him a lamp and the deputy proceeded. "The State of South Carolina, County of Abbeville." He stopped, looked around the courtroom and continued, "The State against Jeff David indictment for murder."

He stopped again and glared at each juror. The deputy took

a deep breath and let out the words as though it was his last breath. Jeff's knees shook. He steadied himself by hanging onto the table in front of him. Jim became pensive waiting. He stood on one leg, then the other.

The deputy read, "Verdict, not guilty. This is the verdict and so say you all."

Each juror assented as Judge Frasier sat with his mouth open, listening to every "yes."

Old Jeff began to smile and weep at the same time. He threw his arms around Jim and cried openly, "De Lord Almighty bless you, de Lord bless you!"

"Jeff, I am so glad, so relieved. Now I don't know what to say except you are free and can go home. Just as a precaution, I am sending you with the sheriff for one more night only. Your wife can go home with you tomorrow. We made it, Jeff, at last, at last!"

Jim could see a few women weeping and some older men smiling openly. These people had been through the entire trial and ordeal. Jim saluted them, for years earlier they shouted, "Boo."

"Jim, wait a minute," said the foreman, Major Wardlaw.

Jim wondered what he wanted and stood up straight before the major, as though he were ready to do battle.

"I want to take a few minutes of your time to tell you something. During the trial I asked the jury not to discuss any part of the case or express an opinion. Everyone agreed, and when they retired to reach a verdict, no one knew how the other would vote."

"That's good, major. Anything else?"

"Yes, Jim. I had each person write his decision on a piece

of paper. Each ballot after it was collected said, 'not guilty.' So, you see, they did not know what the verdict would be until it was announced. They were just as astonished to find all twelve votes in accord."

"That's good news to me."

"We have one more request. If you have no more use for the 12 knives presented as evidence, each one of us on the jury would like one as a souvenir."

"I'll be happy to give each one a knife. Let me get them out of my briefcase and give one to each juror."

Again, Jim headed home earlier that night he had felt the weight of the world on his shoulders, but now everything looked perfectly beautiful to him. He strolled in the darkness, even though he sensed a keen desire to be home and finish the grog left on the table.

"Yes, yes," said Jim raising his hand to the sky. "A great burden has been lifted from my shoulders and an air of relief was imminent in the long four-year fight, with a victory at last. I even sensed a bit of gratitude from the jurors."

At 3 a.m. Jim opened the door of his house and eased himself into his chair. Right by the chair was a fresh drink, and he could hear Lauren coming down the stairs.

"It's good news, my dear. Hurry, it's good news."

CHAPTER 16

Several days elapsed, when Lauren called from the top of the stairs, "Jim, Jim, are you sure you didn't forget anything while you were on your way to the office?"

"No, my dear, I am sure I have forgotten nothing except my hat which I am about to put on."

There was a soft knock at the door, and Jim wondered who it could be at this early hour of the morning. He opened the door and to his surprise saw Jeff, his wife, and son standing on the bottom of the step, looking up at him with their hands folded.

"Good morning, Davids. How are you? Surprised to see you here. I thought you'd be at peace now and free from harm. But it's good to see you. How can I help you this morning?"

"Massa Jim, ah don't know how to tell you, but we's no longer needed, 'cause as you know Massa George and Miz Drusilla is gone, and, well, Massa Gideon says we's no longer can live in da cabin."

"I'm sorry. Can't you find another place? What about your friends here?"

"You sees, Massa Jim, we's got no friends no more. They's 'fraid 'cause…'cause dey say if we's taken in by them, there'll be a lynching. So's, sir, we come to be bond slaves at your service. Massa Jim, we'll do anything for you. Anything. Anything."

"Jeff, I must say that's kind of you, but I must refuse your offer. I don't want you to be my slave. That reasoning should be eliminated forever."

The Davids looked dejected, and Jasper put his hand on his father's shoulder. In the meantime, Lauren came to the bottom of the stairs. She had heard the conversation and called her husband's name. He turned and for a minute and didn't know what to say.

Then Jim got an idea and said, "Look, Jeff. We don't want a lynching. Did you tell anyone that you were coming here?"

"No, Massa Jim, no. Ah can honestly say, nobody, nobody inquired."

The rest of his family shook their heads.

"Then you can stay here in the back in the servant's quarters. We'll keep you busy until I make arrangements for you to go to the relatives you mentioned living in Columbia. How's that?"

"Massa Benet, you's an angel. Praise be da Lord. Praise be."

Miranda took them in with only the belongings on their backs. They did chores willingly, and in a week's time, when Jim was certain that the rumors of lynching had subsided, made arrangements for Jeff and family to travel to Columbia and be with their relatives.

Weeks later, Miranda appeared in Jim's office. She still had her working clothes on and seemed excited. She ran past Billy, who tried to stop her. Jim heard the commotion as she came in and looked up from his work.

"Mr. Jim, you better come home quick," said the maid

excitedly, waving her hands up and down. "Jasper is outside the house. He says he has something for you and won't give it to no one but you. You better come quick, sir."

"My goodness. I can't imagine what he is going to give me. How did he get here?"

"He says he walked and walked and slept in bushes off the road."

When Jim arrived home, there was Jasper, sitting on the ground under a tree. He stood up as soon as Jim appeared and smiled.

"Well, Jasper, you came a long way. Are you alone?"

"Yes, sir. Ah's to give you this. Only you, Massa Jim, only you." He pulled a piece of folded paper from his torn pocket and handed it to Jim. Jim tore off the string and found $17.50.

"Jasper, I am grateful, but I was appointed by the court, and it is our custom when appointed to defend a party not to take a fee. Here, you take this back with you to your father."

"My father wanted you to have this, Massa Jim."

"Tell him I am grateful."

"Yes, suh. I will." Jasper turned, put the money back in his pocket and left the small yard and headed toward the road that would take him back home.

Jim figured the case cost him over $700 not including most of the fee for the detective who had to be paid, and that used up the governor's contingent fund many times over.

Months later the detective did find Sam in Mississippi but lost him. He found his accomplice in Lake City, Florida. Jim expressed his appreciation to Mr. Parry, but with Jeff acquitted, he preferred the case remain closed.

Five years later Sam was seen in southeastern Georgia.

James King reported seeing him to Sam's friends. Jim never returned King's messages or paid a visit to his home. He figured the captain would want a reward for bringing Sam back for a trial. Jim wanted nothing further to do with the case. He summed up the situation in his mind, concluding that destiny works in mysterious ways. Here was an old man found guilty of a double murder and sentenced to death; five times respited; saved from death by lynching and by the sheriff's vigilance; set on a scaffold as a condemned man and tortured to confess he committed the crime; tried a second time and given freedom. In actuality, Jeff would have been hanged six weeks after his first trial, but it all hinged on the petition King gave Jim Benet for the reward that just happened to set off the Decrees for Providence. Oddly enough, that very informal request saved a man's life and the community forever.

Twenty-five years later, Sam returned and opened a store on the south side of Greenwood.